An ADE

MW01258580

BLACKTHORN MANOR
HAUNTING

CHERYL
BRADSHAW

Marriage is neither heaven nor hell, it is simply purgatory.
—Abraham Lincoln

CHAPTER 1

Addison Lockhart had expected to wake on the day of her wedding feeling refreshed, peaceful, and calm. But ever since she'd arrived at Blackthorn Manor the day before, a distressing uneasiness had coursed through her body like an illness determined to spread. She'd tried meditating, tried focusing on wedding preparations. She'd even indulged in a glass of wine. It made no difference. Not only was she unable to quell her worrisome feelings, they persevered and grew stronger.

Even now, sitting on a chair in front of an oval antique mirror, twisting the ends of her long, auburn hair over a curling iron, her hands trembled and she felt anxious, like she wasn't alone, even though no one else was in the room with her. It seemed every nook and cranny inside the manor had eyes, and all of them were watching her every move.

A gust of cool air swept across her back, causing the hair on her neck to stand on end. Startled, she dropped the curling iron and it clattered against the dark hardwood floor below. She reached down and picked it up, gasping when she rose and gazed into the mirror again. She could have sworn she saw something in the mirror's reflection—a shape maybe, or the faint glimmer of an object behind her. It had appeared only for an instant, and then it was gone.

Get a hold of yourself, Addison.

You're working yourself up over nothing.

No one is here.

There's nothing to worry about.

Nothing.

A hand pressed against the small of her back, and she shot out of her chair and whipped around, poised to strike with a hairbrush.

Luke, her fiancé, stood in front of her, his palms in the air. "Whoa, whoa. It's just me. You're really jumpy today. Is everything all right?"

She exhaled a long breath, lowered the hairbrush, and nodded. "I ... yeah, I'm fine."

"Really? Because you looked like you were about to beat me with that brush."

"I'm sorry, Luke. I didn't hear you come in. You're not supposed to see me before the wedding. Bad luck or something."

He leaned toward her, planted a kiss on her forehead, and smiled. "I think we're okay. You're not even dressed yet, and we still have a couple of hours before the ceremony. I thought I'd check in on you and see if I can get you anything."

There *was* something he could do—one thing she wanted more than anything else right now.

"Have you seen my grandmother? Has she arrived yet?"

He shook his head. "I don't think she's here."

Addison sighed. "I tried calling, and she didn't answer. If she's not here soon, she'll miss our wedding."

"She wouldn't miss our wedding. I'm sure she'll be here anytime now. You know Marjorie. She's all about making a grand entrance."

He was right. Marjorie had more flash and flare than women

half her age, and she never missed an opportunity to flaunt it. "When you see her, tell her I need to talk to her, okay?"

He leaned forward, planting a kiss on her forehead. "Will do."

She thought he'd leave the room, but he didn't. He just stood there, staring.

"What is it?" Addison asked.

He shrugged. "I don't know, to be honest. Maybe you can tell me."

"I'm not sure what you mean. Tell you what?"

"On the way here yesterday, you were so happy. Today you seem different, like something's on your mind. Are you second-guessing anything? Should I be worried?"

She reached out, swiping a wisp of his long, sandy-colored bangs out of his eye. No matter how many knots twisted her insides, she wouldn't allow anything to ruin their day. "I've been ready to marry you for a long time, Luke. I can't wait to be your wife."

"If it isn't our wedding, what's bothering you?"

Luke was aware of Addison's gift, her ability to communicate with the spirits of those who had passed on, but she didn't want to worry him. Not today. And besides, there was nothing to confirm her suspicions.

Not yet.

"I haven't eaten anything today," she said. "I'm sure that's all it is."

"What happened to the breakfast the staff sent up this morning?"

"I've been too busy preparing for the wedding to eat it."

Luke glanced around, his eyes coming to rest on a round metal tray. He grabbed it, set it on the dresser next to Addison, and removed the lid, staring at the food like it was no longer appetizing.

"You need to eat something, okay?" he said. "Even if it's a piece a stale toast. I don't want you passing out on me when we're saying our vows."

Addison smiled. "I will. I promise."

"Hey, thanks for agreeing to get married here. I'm sure this place isn't what you had in mind."

He was wrong. It was exactly what she'd had in mind. She had seen her wedding day before, years earlier, in a vision. Not the manor itself, but the ocean in front where they were to be married. She'd seen those in attendance too, and everything had come to pass, just like she knew it would.

She gazed at her hand, at the engagement ring Luke had given her two years ago, a ring once belonging to his grandmother. "It's only fitting we marry at the same place your grandparents did."

"I just thought the owners would have done a better job of preserving the place. The paint, the exterior, the roof—it's all falling apart. I had no idea when I booked it. You deserve better."

"It has sentimental meaning, and that makes it perfect."

He shrugged. "If you say so."

Luke stepped into the hall, closing the door behind him.

Addison walked to the closet and unzipped the plastic cover her wedding dress was wrapped in. She removed the dress, smiling at the slim A-line design she'd worked so hard to fit into over the last few months. She admired it for a moment, and then stared at her face, noticing how nice her makeup looked. She could hardly see the freckles.

Her attention diverted to her bedroom window. A young woman dressed in black stood in front of the manor, gazing at the sea, her hips swaying from side to side as if she were drunk. The woman was unfamiliar and seemed out of place, given they were miles from town, and Addison had been told by the manor's owners that Luke and Addison's small group of family and friends were the only guests staying at the manor for the weekend.

Addison walked toward the window, wondering who the woman was, why she was there, and how she got there in the first place. The dress she wore appeared several decades old, if not older. As if she knew Addison was watching, the woman looked up, meeting her gaze. Before Addison had the chance to open the window and address the woman, someone knocked on her bedroom door.

Thinking it was her grandmother at last, Addison dashed to the door. But she didn't find Marjorie on the other side. She found the woman who owned the manor.

Mrs. Ravencroft had a scowl on her face and a plate in her hands containing two pieces of toast and an assortment of fruit. She tipped her head to the side, glaring at the untouched tray of food on the dresser. "I heard you didn't eat the quiche Whitney sent up this morning."

Addison shook her head. "I didn't. I'm sorry."

Mrs. Ravencroft pressed her eyes closed like she had no time for Addison's excuses. "Your loss. The three-cheese quiche won an award last year for the best breakfast dish in the county."

"I am sorry. I'm sure it's amazing."

"Your fiancé asked me to bring you a fresh plate. I agreed to it, but only this one time. I do not appreciate the food I prepare going to waste."

"I didn't mean to—"

"It doesn't matter now. Just take it."

Mrs. Ravencroft shoved the plate into Addison's hands, brushed past her, and scooped the tray off the dresser, before walking back out of the room.

"Wait just a minute," Addison said. "Can I ask you a question?"

Mrs. Ravencroft sighed. "What is it?"

"You said there were no other guests staying here this weekend, right?"

"There are not. It's only your wedding party."

"What about staff?"

"My husband and I tend to the rooms ourselves, for the most part. Whitney is the chef, and aside from the gardener, she's the only staff I have. She lives in one of the guesthouses behind the manor with her husband Colin."

Addison guessed Mrs. Ravencroft was in her late seventies, so it was a shock to hear she did all of the housework and tended to the guests herself.

Mrs. Ravencroft crossed her arms. "Why are you asking about other guests?"

"There's a woman outside. I don't recognize her."

Addison turned and pointed, only to realize the woman she'd seen was gone.

Mrs. Ravencroft glanced out the window, irritated. "Well, she's not there now, is she? Are you sure it wasn't someone from *your* wedding party? From this distance, it could have been anyone."

The *distance* Mrs. Ravencroft had referred to wasn't far, and even if it was, at times one of Addison's gifts was binocular vision. Sometimes she saw herself as an owl in her dreams and visions.

"The woman was right in front of the manor, staring out into the ocean," Addison said.

"Whitney walks along the beach every day. Perhaps you saw her."

Whitney's hair was a different color than the woman she'd seen through the window. It couldn't have been her. "There was a longing in the woman's eyes, almost like she wished the ocean would open and swallow her up."

"*Swallow her up*? What an odd thing to say."

Addison supposed she was right, and since the woman was no longer in view, it no longer mattered. "Thanks for bringing another plate of food. I'll eat it this time."

Mrs. Ravencroft smirked, pausing a moment in the doorway. "I'm just curious. What did the woman you saw look like?"

"She was tall and slim. She wore a black dress that went to her feet, and she had long, dark hair. Her skin was pale, almost white, and even though she seemed distraught, she was beautiful."

Addison detected a look of uneasiness in Mrs. Ravencroft's eyes, though she did her best to hide it. She averted her eyes and said, "I'll leave you to get ready, Miss Lockhart."

She then closed the door behind her.

Addison took a few bites of toast and set the plate down. She walked to the window and opened it, peering across the shoreline. In the distance, she thought she saw the silhouette of the woman she'd seen before, but the woman was too far away now. It was hard to know for sure.

Hoping to get a better look, Addison leaned out over the windowsill, gasping when she felt an intense pressure against her back—someone thrusting her forward. Addison grabbed the side of the window to brace herself, but it was too late. She was already falling.

CHAPTER 2

Addison regained consciousness, her eyes opening to a small audience huddled over her. Luke. Luke's parents. Her father. Her grandmother Marjorie. Her closest friend Lia McReedy, and an irritated-looking Mrs. Ravencroft.

"Are you all right?" Luke asked. "You fainted."

Addison nodded. "I think so."

But he was wrong. She hadn't fainted.

She stared up at the window she'd just fallen from, perplexed. She'd landed on her backside on the porch, and yet she felt fine. No bruises. No broken bones. No injuries.

How could I have fallen without getting hurt?

It's a two-story drop.

It isn't possible.

Luke knelt down, extending a hand toward her. She took it, and he pulled her to a standing position.

"I need a minute," she said.

"Are you hurt?" he asked.

"I'm just shaken up. Did anyone see what happened?"

No one had.

"I was inside the house and heard a noise outside," Luke said. "I opened the door and found you passed out on the porch, which was strange, since I never saw you leave your room."

"I didn't," she said.

"What do you mean?"

Addison pointed to the open window, and everyone looked up.

"I fell from the window. I'm just not sure how. The last thing I remember is opening it and leaning out. Then I was falling."

Mrs. Ravencroft snickered a laugh. "Don't be ridiculous. There's no way you fell from the window. You couldn't have."

"I'm not a liar."

Mrs. Ravencroft grabbed Addison's hands, looked her over. "It's not possible. You don't have a scratch on you. I noticed an empty glass of wine on the dresser when I came to your room. Perhaps you've had too much today?"

Marjorie stepped in front of Mrs. Ravencroft, wagging a pointy, blood-red fingernail in her face. "Perhaps you should consider watching what you say to *my* granddaughter."

"And perhaps *you* or someone in your party should keep a better eye on her today. She's obviously intoxicated."

"It was *one* glass of wine," Addison said, "two hours ago."

Mrs. Ravencroft threw her hands in the air. "I'm not doing this. Not my circus."

She pivoted and went inside the house, slamming the door behind her.

Marjorie smirked, grabbed the handle on her suitcase, and glanced around, her head shaking. "Look at this place. It's falling apart. It's not fit for visitors, and it's definitely not suitable for my granddaughter's wedding."

"Gran, it's fine," Addison said. "This place has special meaning to Luke."

"I don't care what it has. It's a dump. And what's the matter with you? Why are you thrusting yourself out of bedroom windows? When did you become so clumsy?"

As all eyes fell on her, Addison considered her answer. "You're right. I lost my balance, I guess. It's my fault. I should have been more careful."

Marjorie frowned. "It isn't your fault, dearest. This place is a death trap, and you shouldn't allow that woman to—"

Addison squeezed Marjorie's hand. "There's less than an hour before the wedding. I've been waiting for you to get here before I change into my dress. Will you help me?"

Marjorie nodded and followed Addison into the house. Once they were out of earshot, she grabbed Addison's arm. "I want to know what's *really* going on, Addison. I saw the look you just gave me. If you expect me to believe you shot out of that window, I don't."

Addison walked to the staircase, tapping a finger to her own lips. "Lower your voice, Gran."

"Why should I?"

"Please. Let's get to my room first. I'll explain everything."

They reached the room, and Addison closed the door, startled to find an unfamiliar man inside, arranging a large display of flowers inside a vase on the dresser. He was a slender man of about fifty and had sandy-blond shoulder-length hair swept back into a ponytail. He was dressed in all black, including black rubber bracelets on his wrists.

Marjorie stepped in front of Addison like a protective shield. "Excuse me. Who are you, and why are you in my granddaughter's room?"

He wiped a wet hand on his pant leg, stuck his hand out to Addison, and they shook. "Sorry, I didn't mean to startle you. I'm Brad, the Ravencroft's gardener. She told me you were getting married today, and I thought I'd bring up some flowers from the garden."

"What kind of establishment are they running here?" Marjorie glared at Brad. "You should ask permission before entering a guest's room."

"I wanted the flowers to be a surprise," Brad said. "I didn't mean to upset anyone."

"My grandmother's right," Addison said. "You should have said something. But I appreciate the gesture. Thank you."

He nodded, made a second apology, and hurried out of the room.

"That man looks like he's on his way to a punk-rock funeral," Marjorie said. "I can't believe they hired him."

"Gran, he seems nice. You're judging him, and you don't even know him."

"You're quite naïve sometimes, Addison. Now let's move on. What did you want to tell me?"

Knowing the house was old and the ease in which voices carried, Addison lowered her voice, tipping her head toward the other end of the room. "Let's go in the bathroom where there's an additional degree of privacy, at least."

Marjorie shrugged. "Fine."

Addison shut the bathroom door behind them and leaned against it. "You're right. I didn't fall out of the window—I was pushed."

Marjorie folded her arms. "What do you mean *pushed*? Explain yourself."

Addison described what had occurred since she'd arrived at the manor.

When she finished, Marjorie said, "I suppose the biggest question we need to address now is, who do you think pushed you? Someone living or someone dead?"

Addison considered the question. "I'm not sure. When I leaned out the window and felt the hand on my back, it felt real. I wanted to turn, see who was behind me, but there wasn't time. All I could do was grab the window and try to keep from falling. When I realized there was nothing I could do to stop it from happening, I closed my eyes and braced myself. And then the strangest thing happened. Right before I landed, it felt like I'd been wrapped in a protective cloud, like someone was holding me, protecting me from slamming into the porch."

Marjorie leaned against the wall. "Spirits, even the most evil ones, can mess with your mind. They can taunt you, make you feel afraid and unsafe, but in my experience, they can't harm you. Only the living has the power to do that."

"How can you be sure?"

"Decades of experience, I guess. I'll explain it to you the way my mother did to me. The abilities we have were given to us for a reason. Our family was chosen. At certain times, we're protected. I don't know how or why. We just are. Call it the blessing within the curse."

"I see no blessing in any of it. Today is my wedding day. All I wanted was one day—one single, peaceful day—where I could be free from all of it."

Marjorie backed against the counter. "What do you know about this place? You said the manor had special meaning to Luke because of his grandparents. Why?"

"Didn't you get the letter I sent you a few weeks ago? I explained everything."

Marjorie nodded. "I got it. I just … well … I was running late for brunch with a friend, so I have to admit I merely skimmed through it. I meant to look it over again later and didn't. Sorry."

"Luke's grandparents were married here."

"I understand the sentimentality, but this place …" Marjorie scratched a fingernail along the peeling, floral-textured wallpaper on the bathroom wall. "The whole thing—it's in decay."

"So was Grayson Manor when I inherited it," Addison said. "And look at it now. Luke has restored it to what it was like when you lived there."

"I suppose it doesn't matter either way. We're here now. We need to make the best of it."

"I could have chosen another place to get married," Addison said. "I almost did."

"What stopped you?"

"I saw this place in a vision a few years ago, and I knew I was supposed to get married here. But now, I can't help but wonder if … I mean, it just seems like …"

She stopped herself. She didn't want to say it. Didn't want to think it. She hadn't seen a spirit in several months. Why now? Why today?

"You're meant to do more here than just get married," Marjorie said. "I felt it the moment I drove through the gates to this place. It was subtle, but it was there. Who else knows what you just told me?"

"No one."

"Good. It's just as well. Whether living or dead, someone doesn't want you here. We need to find out who and why. For now, it will have to wait. It's still your day, and I'm not about to let anyone or any*thing* ruin it. Let's get you married."

CHAPTER 3

Addison stepped outside and breathed in a lungful of crisp sea air. The day's turmoil and stress melted away, replaced with warmth and ardor, and an overwhelming sense of gratitude and adoration for Luke, a man who had always loved her without limitation.

Nothing more will ruin this day.

Not one thing.

Lia joined her, her dark-brown, bob-style hair bouncing as she descended the steps. She inspected Addison's gown and said, "Wow, Addy, you look beautiful."

With Lia's fondness for dark leggings and simple shirts, Addison had never seen her in a dress before, and based on the way Lia kept yanking the sides down to smooth it out, Addison assumed she probably wouldn't see her in a dress again anytime soon.

She squeezed Lia's hand. "You look gorgeous in your dress."

"Really? Because I feel like an enormous pink whale. It took ten minutes to get the zipper all the way up. Last week I was thinking I needed to lose about five pounds, and now I'm thinking it's more like twenty."

"Well, you look amazing, and I'm glad you're here. Once the wedding is over, we need to find some time to talk later."

Lia raised a brow. "Is everything all right?"

Addison shook her head. "There isn't time to explain right now, or I'd fill you in."

Lia stared at Addison a moment. "Oh no. You've seen something, haven't you? You have the same look on your face that you had the night we first met—the night I arrived at your house to look at the bone you found."

Addison grinned, recalling their first encounter. "We didn't exactly hit it off on day one, did we?"

"I was in work mode, and you were a suspect. I'm just glad we took the time to get to know each other."

"Me too."

"So … *have* you *seen* something?"

Addison nodded. "It's hard to explain. I haven't made contact with anyone yet, but something is about to happen. I can feel it. And it's all tied to the manor somehow."

Before Addison could elaborate, her father joined them, his face beaming as he reached for Addison's hand, entwining her arm around his own. "It's time. Are you ready?"

Arm in arm, Addison walked toward Luke, joining him in front of the pastor at the water's edge. The pastor welcomed those who had gathered and offered his own heartfelt words about marriage. Luke recited his vows, and then it was Addison's turn.

"I, Addison, take you, Luke, to be my lawfully wedded husband, to have and to hold, from this day forward, for better, for worse, for richer, for poorer, in sickness and in health, in this life, and in the next."

"*In the next*" was a phrase Addison had added herself, favoring it to the traditional words "*till death do us part.*" After all she'd seen and experienced over the last few years, she no longer believed life ended when the physical body was put to rest. The soul lived on. People lived on. Couples reunited together. There *was* a "next."

Luke took Addison's hand, rubbing his thumb across her palm. The minister offered a few final words and then nodded at Luke, indicating his permission for Luke to embrace his new bride. Luke leaned forward and cupped Addison's chin in his hand, sealing their vows with a kiss.

As Addison wrapped her arms around Luke's neck, she noticed an unexpected guest in their midst. Hovering a few feet behind her father was the woman in black. They locked eyes, and Addison clenched her jaw, forcing herself to remain calm. Finally able to see the woman up close, Addison noticed she was young, probably in her mid-twenties. The black dress was dated, but Addison was unable to determine the era. As Addison stared at the woman, absorbing her energy, her emotions changed from light and happy to heavy and forlorn, like the intense, crushing weight of an automobile compactor, flattening her until she was razor thin.

What had the woman suffered to cause such a grave amount of pain?

Parting from Luke's embrace, Addison's eyes remained on the woman. A single tear rolled down the woman's cheek. Then another. Addison wanted to reach out, to speak to her, but she couldn't. Not now, not in front of her guests.

Addison's father stepped forward, shaking hands with Luke, offering his congratulations. Marjorie looked at Addison's face and turned, like she understood what her granddaughter must be experiencing.

Luke's mother threw her arms around Addison and said, "Welcome to the family. We're so happy for you both."

Luke's father thumbed in his wife's direction and nodded. "What she said. I don't know about the rest of you, but I'm starved."

"The dining room is all set up, and dinner should be ready," Luke said.

Luke's father nodded. "Great. I'll lead the way."

He turned, plowing through the ghostly apparition like she was nothing more than invisible air, and all Addison could do was stand there, watching the woman dissipate into a fine mist.

CHAPTER 4

Dinner was served in a small, but elaborate ballroom in the basement level of the manor, which Mrs. Ravencroft explained had been sealed off to most guests over the years, thus allowing its original charm to remain intact. A trio of iron and glass-bead chandeliers graced the center of a pressed-metal ceiling, which had been painted white, giving it the appearance of ornate plaster. And although Addison noticed a few threadlike cobwebs, the overall elegance of the room, combined with the amazing floral arrangements Brad had put together, made her feel like a princess stepping into a ballroom for the first time.

An antique Victor wind-up phonograph played Frank Sinatra's "Like Someone in Love," the perfect song for a first dance together. Luke twirled Addison around the center of the room, and when the song faded to an end and was replaced with another, he handed Addison off to her father, who was patiently standing off to the side, waiting his turn.

Grabbing his daughter's hand, her father said, "I wish your mother could have been here to see you get married today. She would have been so proud."

"I've thought of her many times today," Addison said, "and what it would have been like if she could have been by my side. A few times I even thought I sensed her presence."

"Maybe you did. Wherever she is, I'm sure she's smiling down upon the woman you've become, and the happiness you've found in your life. She would have approved of Luke."

Addison smiled. "I think so too."

Her father clutched her hands a bit tighter. "Is … umm … is everything all right?"

"Of course it is, Dad. Why wouldn't it be?"

"You've been all smiles since the wedding, but earlier I noticed you biting the inside of your cheek. Haven't seen you do that in a while. You used to do it all the time when you were a child, whenever you were nervous. Do you remember?"

Of course she did.

She'd have to be a lot more careful.

A lot more aware.

"I'm fine. Truly. I'm sure it was just a few butterflies before the wedding. I feel great now. I'm a lot more relaxed."

He leaned back and looked into her eyes, searching. "You sure? Is there anything you want to tell me, because you know you can always talk to me, no matter what's on your—"

"I know, Dad. I'm good, okay? You don't need to worry."

He stared at her for a time, and she could tell he was unconvinced, but he let it go and moved on. "This place seems to have a lot of history. I was in the parlor earlier, looking at the old family photos hanging on the wall. I thought to myself, 'I've never seen such somber portraits before.' No one appears happy."

"Most people didn't smile in old photos. Someone once told me it was because smiling indicated the person was vulgar—lewd or mad, prone to loud outbursts or a drunkard. Hard to believe people read so much into a simple smile back then."

"Makes me think this place is crawling with spirits, ancestors of the woman who runs it. Has anything *happened* since we've been here? You know ... have you *seen* anything out of the ordinary?"

Addison paused, unsure how to answer the question. She didn't like lying to her father, but she didn't want to worry him, either. But it was obvious he had used the family photos as an opening. When she took longer than usual to answer, he pulled back, blinked at her. "You have, haven't you? You've seen someone. I can tell. When? Where?"

"Earlier today. It's nothing to worry about. Nothing I can't handle."

Several feet away, Marjorie danced with Luke. Addison glanced in her direction until they locked eyes, and then she tipped her head toward the door. Marjorie nodded.

"I'm going to take a walk with Gran before it gets too dark," Addison said. "Thank you for the dance, Dad. I love you."

She kissed her father's cheek and made a beeline for Luke.

"I'm going for a walk along the beach," she said. "Not long, just for a few minutes."

He grinned. "I was just thinking of how nice it would be to take a walk together."

"Actually, Gran asked if she could go with me. I think there's something she needs to talk to me about. Why don't we get up early in the morning and watch the sunrise instead?"

Luke glanced out the window and frowned. "It's getting dark out. But all right. If that's what you want to do."

Addison wrapped her hands around his neck. "I won't be long, and then we can spend the rest of the night together."

He bent toward her ear, and whispered, "I look forward to it."

Addison grabbed her lace shawl off the back of the chair, threw it around herself, and met Marjorie outside. It was dusk, Addison's favorite time of day, the moment when the sun's rays cascaded across the ocean's surface in a glittery display of effulgent light. She stared at the calm stillness of the ocean and breathed it in.

"Where to?" Marjorie asked.

"There's a lookout spot not far from here I'd like to check out," Addison replied.

"I imagine your interest has to do with the woman you saw earlier."

"She walked there earlier and then stopped, looking out at sea."

"You're lucky, you know."

"How so?" Addison asked.

"Your visions allow you to see a lot farther than I ever have been able to. I'm sure it's because your spirit animal is an owl, and mine's a crow, of all things."

Addison cupped a hand over her mouth.

"Go on," Marjorie said. "Have a good laugh. I did too the first time I shifted."

"Crows *are* considered one of the smartest birds in the world. At least you're not a vulture."

"True, although it's of little comfort."

"What was my mother?"

"Your mother was one of the most magnificent of birds, an eagle, which would have suited her well had she not refused to become a medium." Marjorie sighed and placed a hand on her hip. "Not you, though. You've welcomed it, and so will your daughter."

"My … daughter?"

Marjorie turned to Addison and winked. "Would you like to know what spirit animal she is?"

"How could you know? She hasn't been born yet. I'm not even pregnant."

"Best start preparing for her now, dearest. The sooner the better."

Best start preparing for her now?

Addison and Luke had taken precautions so she wouldn't become pregnant yet. They wanted some time together as a married couple first. A year or two. Maybe even more.

"You still have a great deal to learn about the power you possess," Marjorie said.

"There's more? More than I already know?"

"Oh, yes. Much more."

"Why are you only telling me this now?"

"You only started using and understanding your abilities a few years ago. You needed time to get used to them, time to learn all the things you're capable of doing."

"You should have just told me," Addison said. "I could have handled ..."

Addison's words trailed off. Several feet in front of her, the woman in black appeared.

"You were saying?" Marjorie asked.

Addison tapped Marjorie on the wrist. "It's her. The woman I saw earlier. The woman in black."

Marjorie nodded but said nothing.

Addison pointed. "She's there, right in front of us. Don't you see her?"

Marjorie nodded, her eyes following Addison's finger.

Marjorie's behavior seemed strange and aloof.

Why hadn't she also acknowledged the woman?

Did she not see what Addison saw?

The sun had almost been extinguished, leaving only the faintest glimmer of light. Addison stared into the woman's lifeless, melancholy eyes. "I want to help you. Will you let me? Will you tell me why you're still here?"

The woman stared out to sea, refusing to acknowledge Addison's presence.

"You obviously summoned me," Addison said. "You want me to know you're here. What do you need from me?"

Looking over the edge of the cliff, the woman watched the waves crash against the rocks like hand grenades, causing one explosion after another.

Addison shook her head at Marjorie. "She won't talk to me. I don't know what to do. I have no idea how to help her."

"Perhaps it's not time yet."

"She clearly wants something. How much time could she possibly need?"

Marjorie squeezed Addison's shoulder. "She might be afraid to connect with you, but when she's ready, you'll know. If you see her, it's because she wants you to. I know this isn't what you want to hear, but this one might take a little more time than the others."

Gran was right.

It *wasn't* the answer she wanted.

The wedding was over, and she'd tired of this place.

Addison turned back toward the woman, who was now teetering on the cliff's edge.

"Joseph," the woman whispered.

Instinct told Addison what would happen next. And though she was helpless to change the outcome, she reached out, attempting to grab the woman's arm. But there was nothing she could do to save her, nothing to keep her from her fate, a fate that had been set in motion long ago, long before Addison ever stepped foot on the estate at Blackthorn Manor.

The woman spread her arms to the side and stepped off the edge, her dress flapping in the wind as her body soared downward, crashing like a rag doll onto the jagged, unforgiving rocks below.

CHAPTER 5

Addison drifted close to the cliff's edge, her frame feeble and limp.

Rattled.

Fingers gripped her arm, reeling her backward.

"What in the hell are you doing?" Marjorie asked. "One more step and you would have gone over."

"The woman. Did you see her? She committed suicide … just now … a few feet from where we're standing. She just spread her arms and walked right off the edge."

"At least you know *how* she died. Now you just need to figure out what she's still doing here."

Addison wrenched herself free from Marjorie's grip. "You didn't answer my question. You nodded when I asked if you saw her, but you *didn't* see her, did you?"

"Don't be ridiculous. Of course I did."

"Describe her to me then. What does her hair look like? What color are her eyes?"

Before Marjorie could respond, an unfamiliar male voice said, "Beautiful night tonight, isn't it?"

Marjorie and Addison spun around. A middle-aged couple headed in their direction. Their hands were entwined, bare feet coated in sand. The man stood a foot taller than the woman and had a round face and short, salt-and-pepper hair with a touch of curl to it. The woman was petite and had auburn hair that fell just below her shoulders.

"Hi, I'm Colin," the man said. "And this is my wife Whitney. Congratulations on your wedding today."

"Thank you." Addison looked at Whitney. "You're the chef here, right?"

Whitney nodded.

"And you both live in the guesthouse on the estate," Addison added.

"One of them," Colin said. "There are two. It's beautiful here. We love living by the ocean."

"And you have no children?"

"I, umm, I can't have them," Whitney said.

"I'm sorry," Addison said. "I shouldn't have asked. It was—"

"No, no," Whitney said. "It's fine, really. We've come to terms with it. I mean … *I* have come to terms with it. I was married once before, and let's just say the topic of kids was one of the biggest strains on our marriage. Then one day my ex announced he was going to be a father. He'd been seeing another woman on the side. He left me to be with her. Now they're married and have two kids of their own."

"Bastard," Marjorie said.

"*Gran!*" Addison chided.

"She's right," Whitney said. "He was a real dirt bag. The best part is, I met Colin because of it, and now when I look back, I realize it was meant to be."

"What do you do, Colin?" Addison asked.

He slid an arm over Whitney's shoulder. "I flip houses."

"That's similar to what Luke does. He restores them."

"Yeah, we were talking earlier today. He showed me a bunch of before-and-after photos of your place. I wish I had his talent."

Addison glanced at her phone, checking the time. "Speaking of Luke, I need to get back. I promised I wouldn't be gone long."

"Great to meet you both," Whitney said. "I left a bottle of champagne on your bed, a couple of glasses, and a few other treats I thought you might like. If there's anything else you need, let me know."

CHAPTER 6

Addison tossed and turned in bed. It was just after one o'clock in the morning, and her mind refused to shut down, mostly because she wouldn't let it. Part of her kept thinking of the woman. The other part kept reliving the moment she was pushed from the window, which had her worried about what else might happen if she dozed off. Even with her grandmother's assurances about spirits being incapable of harm, she still wasn't sure it had been a spirit.

Addison stared at Luke's masculine yet kind face. He looked so peaceful sleeping there next to her. Telling him about what happened earlier would put him on edge, so she decided it was best to wait for now. She peeled back the covers and crept out of bed, her movements slow, so as not to wake him.

It was the perfect time to do some digging, and she knew the exact place to start: the parlor where much of the manor's history was kept. She made her way downstairs, startled when she turned the corner and found Mrs. Ravencroft still awake, sitting by a crackling fire, perusing a book. She considered backing out of the room, until the wood floor beneath her creaked, giving her away.

Mrs. Ravencroft glanced up and snapped the book closed, setting it on the table next to her.

"I'm sorry," Addison said. "I didn't mean to disturb you."

Mrs. Ravencroft raised a brow. "You didn't."

Addison shifted her attention to the portraits on the wall, the ones her father mentioned earlier. One stood out in particular. A man standing next to a woman, an unmistakable woman whose eyes were dark and longing—the woman in black.

Not wanting to linger too long, Addison turned to Mrs. Ravencroft. "I didn't think anyone would be awake."

"I don't sleep much anymore. Three, four hours a night if I'm lucky. But you, you're young. Why haven't you gone to bed yet?"

"I did. I couldn't sleep, so I—"

Mrs. Ravencroft narrowed her eyes. "Why are you sneaking around at this hour?"

"I'm not sneak—"

"Of course you are. Shouldn't you be with your husband?"

Seeking a diversion, Addison pointed at the book on the table. "What are you reading?"

"Bronte."

Addison crossed the room and stuck her hands out, warming them by the fire. "Charlotte or Emily?"

"Emily."

Emily—the more melancholy of the Bronte sisters. It came as no surprise. "I'm familiar."

"Isn't everyone?"

"I read *Wuthering Heights* in high school," Addison said.

"And what did you think of it?"

"I thought it was … interesting."

Mrs. Ravencroft swished a hand through the air. "*Interesting* is such a dull word, you know. It's little better than saying the book was nothing out of the ordinary. If you've read it as you say you have, you know it's much more than that."

Addison accepted the slap to the face and moved on. "What do you like about it?"

Mrs. Ravencoft eyed Addison in such a way as to let her know she was well aware of Addison's attempt at small talk.

"It isn't the book I care for as much as Emily herself. There are pieces of her in the story. She was a quiet sort of woman. Reclusive. Logical. Rare. Intelligent. Reminds me of myself, you know."

She had left out another accurate, descriptive word. Emily Bronte was also *troubled*, something Addison didn't dare say aloud.

"Do you read every night?" Addison asked.

"Is this what you *really* want to ask me? I get the feeling it isn't."

"What do you mean?"

"You've been skittish since you've arrived here—curious and bursting with questions. Why not say what's on your mind?"

Addison bit her lip, contemplating how far she could push before Mrs. Ravencroft shut her down like she had before. "How long has the manor been in your family?"

"My grandfather Luther built it. He passed it down to my father Clayton, and when he died, he left it to me, for the most part. I never expected to keep it this long. I always thought I'd sell the place."

"Why?"

"With exception of one or two things, I have no sentimental attachment to it anymore, and I've always thought it was too big for a family of three."

A family of three indicated she had a son or daughter.

"Why didn't you sell it?"

"My husband Gene likes living by the sea, and he's fond of this place. He convinced me to turn it into a bed-and-breakfast so we could profit from all of the wasted space, the rooms we never use. It was a brilliant idea, and it's served us well. But we're not young like we once were, and over the last year, I've grown tired of tending to it. I'm getting too old. The time has finally come to rid myself of it."

"If you leave the manor, where will you go?" Addison asked.

"What difference is it to you?"

"Why not leave it to your son or daughter?"

Mrs. Ravencroft glared at Addison. "Why did you tell everyone you fell from the window earlier today?"

"Because I did."

"If you don't want to say what really happened, it's your choice, I suppose. But there's no reason to lie about it."

"How can you be so sure I lied? Where were *you* when it happened?"

Mrs. Ravencroft leaned forward, folding her arms in front of her. "What are you suggesting?"

"If you didn't see what happened, then you don't know I'm not telling the truth."

"I was in the kitchen at the time. But it doesn't mean I'm not right."

Mrs. Ravencroft rose from the chair and grabbed a poker out of a metal can. She stabbed at the wood, breaking it into pieces. "You should return to bed, to your husband."

She crossed in front of Addison and walked out of the room, pausing before turning the corner. When Addison remained, she sighed and then whipped around. "Come on then, let's go."

"I'd like to stay here for a while if you don't mind."

"I *do* mind. Just because you're a guest here doesn't mean you have a run of the house."

"Has anyone ever died here?"

"By *died*, you mean what exactly?"

The question had seemed self-explanatory.

Apparently she would have to spell it out.

"Has anyone ever committed suicide at the manor, or on the grounds, or at the lookout point by the ocean?"

It seemed to catch Mrs. Ravencroft off-guard. Seconds passed. Addison waited for an answer, listening to the clicking of the clock on the mantel.

Tick. Tock. Tick. Tock.

"Why would you ask such a question?"

"I thought I read something about a tragedy happening here once," Addison said.

Mrs. Ravencroft glanced at the wall like she had gone somewhere else in her mind, locked in a memory she'd rather forget.

"Please," Addison said. "I need to know if a woman threw herself over the edge of the cliff at the lookout point several decades ago."

"Whatever you've heard, forget it. People in this town love to chatter."

"I know you know what happened," Addison said. "What I don't know is why you won't tell me."

Addison walked to the opposite side of the room, snatching the portrait off the wall. She held it out to Mrs. Ravencroft. "This is the woman I saw through my bedroom window this morning. She's dead, isn't she? Who is she to you? Your sister? A relative? Your brother's wife?"

Mrs. Ravencroft tore the portrait out of Addison's hands and hung it back on the wall. She flipped the switch in the room, leaving Addison with nothing but the dying embers of the fire for light.

"I'll put the hall light on to guide you back to your room," Mrs. Ravencroft said. "Goodnight, Mrs. Flynn."

31

CHAPTER 7

Catherine Ravencroft closed the closet door, tugging on a thin piece of string dangling from the ceiling until it clicked, illuminating the area with light. Standing on the tips of her toes, she reached for a small box she kept on the top shelf. It was old and black and dusty—so dusty her fingerprints left oily imprints on the outside when she touched it. She grabbed a sweater she no longer wore from of a hanger and wiped the box down, discarding the sweater inside a wicker hamper. Box in hand, she sat on the floor, staring at the lid.

She wanted to lift it off.

She just couldn't bring herself to do it.

Ever since she'd first set eyes on Addison the day before, a strange feeling had come over the house, almost like the manor had taken on a life of its own. As preposterous as it seemed, Catherine couldn't deny the fact that Addison's presence had shifted the energy somehow, stirring things up that had long been asleep.

It was a problem.

There was something "off" about Addison—something peculiar in her deep-hazel eyes—an odd curiosity, leaving Catherine with more questions than answers.

Why had Addison invented the story about falling from the window the day before? She had to have known that no one would believe her.

How could they?

It would have been impossible to survive such a drop without sustaining a few broken bones, at the very least.

And yet, Catherine's curiosity had been piqued, so when Addison and her guests had headed to the beach for the wedding ceremony, Catherine snuck up to Addison's room, opened the window, and looked out. What she saw surprised her. Three of the roof's shingles in front of the window had slid out of place, and Catherine was certain they had been intact only days before. There hadn't been any storms or gusts of wind in recent days, nothing to explain why the shingles had shifted.

It didn't make any sense.

And why had Addison pointed at the portrait of Cora minutes ago, claiming she'd seen her walking along the beach?

She couldn't have.

It wasn't possible.

Curling a hand over the lid of the box, she hesitated once more. It had been years since she last looked inside—years since she'd allowed the painful flashbacks of the past to creep back into her life. But now she felt as though there was nothing she could do to stop it. Addison had ripped opened the door to her heart, a door she'd kept sealed for so long. Only the tiniest of droplets had made their way out from time to time, but now … now the memories were rushing back.

The floodgates had opened.

Catherine pulled the lid back, discarding it on the floor next to her. She reached inside and pulled out a pair of boy's shoes. They were small and brown, scuffed from daily use. Running her fingers along the worn leather, she could almost see him now, his ball in hand, running circles around her in the yard. She pressed the shoes to her chest, holding them there for a time. Then she set them to the side and reached back into the box. This time she removed a framed photo of a boy dressed in his Sunday best, standing in front of the manor, smiling.

He'd always had such a pleasant disposition.

The closet door creaked open, and Catherine's husband poked his head inside. "Honey? What are you doing in here? Are you all right?"

"I'm fine. I couldn't sleep. I was just reminiscing on old times."

Gene glanced down at the photo in Catherine's hand. "It's been a while since we've looked at this stuff, hasn't it?"

"Too long. Far too long."

"You look tired. Come to bed."

Catherine nodded and returned the shoes back to the box, but she kept the framed photo in her hand. "How do you feel about putting this back on the dresser again?"

He held out a hand, and she took it.

"I think it's a wonderful idea," he said.

"Have you had much interaction with the young woman who got married yesterday?"

He shook his head. "Not really. She's said hello a few times in passing. She seems like a nice girl. Why do you ask?"

"She knows things."

"What things?"

"Things about our past," Catherine said. "Things about Cora."

"How could she? She said she's never been here before."

"I'm not sure yet. But in the morning, she has to go."

CHAPTER 8

Addison stood outside of Marjorie's bedroom door, knocking lightly so she wouldn't disturb the rest of the house. When Marjorie didn't respond, she twisted the knob and looked inside. Gran was curled on her side on the bed, dressed in a pale-pink chiffon nightgown that reminded Addison of one Elizabeth Taylor had worn in the movie *Elephant Walk*. She seemed peaceful, and though Addison wanted to tell her about her encounter with Mrs. Ravencroft, she decided it was best not to disturb her until the morning.

Addison backed out of the room, resigned to return to bed until a faint glow coming from beneath a bedroom door caught her eye. It was a room unoccupied by anyone else in the house. She cracked the door open and stepped inside, finding the room to be similar to others in the house, a relic frozen in time. A small twin bed covered in a blue-and-red plaid quilt rested in the center of the room. Three teddy bears sat on top. There were two nightstands and a dresser, and a closet full of little boy's clothing.

"Hi," a young voice said.

Addison whipped around. Standing a few feet in front of her was a child, a boy no older than seven. He had dark-brown hair and large, playful, brown eyes. He was dressed reminiscent of the '70s in a pair of blue, wide-legged pants, a plaid button-up shirt, a thick, white belt, and brown Buster Brown shoes.

But his clothes weren't what stood out the most. Addison could see right through him.

The boy waved.

Addison waved back.

"I'm Billy," he said. "What's your name?"

"Addison."

Billy's nose wrinkled. "Allison?"

"Close. Addison, with a D."

"That's a funny name. I never met a girl named Addison before."

"When I was your age, my friends called me Addy. How old are you?"

"Six and one quarter."

Addison wondered whether or not Billy was aware he wasn't alive, and decided it would be best to start with a few simple questions first. "Shouldn't you be in bed?"

He shrugged. "I'm not tired."

"Maybe if you put your pajamas on and get under the covers, you would be."

"Nah. I never get sleepy anymore."

"What are you doing up so late?"

"Waiting."

"What are you waiting for?"

Billy blinked, but didn't answer the question. "Will you play with me? No one plays with me anymore. No one has played with me for a long time."

Addison moved closer. "Sure, what would you like to play?"

Billy presented a red ball he'd been concealing behind his back and sat down. "We can only play tonight."

"Why only tonight?"

"I have to go soon."

"Where are you going?"

"Away. Somewhere far from here, I think."

Billy stared at the bedroom door, and his face turned white. "Shh. Someone is coming."

"Who's coming?" Addison whispered.

Billy pressed a finger to his lips, prompting Addison to stop talking. The house was quiet. Not even a single creak in the floor was heard. Could he have been talking about a spirit?

After a minute, Billy said, "I think it's okay now. The bad person is gone."

"Who's the bad person, Billy?"

He shook his head. "I'm not supposed to tell."

"Why not?"

"She told me not to tell."

"Who told you?"

Billy sat down. "I'll roll the ball to you. Then you roll it back. 'Kay?"

Addison nodded and crossed her legs in front of her on the floor, wondering if there was a better way to get Billy to answer her questions. And then one presented itself. "I have an idea. Every time I roll the ball back to you, I get to ask you a question, and you have to answer it. Sound fair?"

He shrugged. "Guess so."

Billy rolled the ball. Addison reached out to grab it. The moment it grazed her hand, the room began spinning, colors swirling like liquid in a blender. First blue, then gray, then black. Lightheaded, Addison closed her eyes. When she opened them, she found herself in the same room she was in before. The furniture was the same, but the room looked different now. It was almost evening, and everything was clean. The walls were no longer dingy and instead were coated in fresh blue paint. Billy was gone, but she wasn't alone. A woman sat on the edge of the bed, her head in her hands.

"Hello," Addison said. "Can you hear me?"

The woman didn't look up, didn't acknowledge her.

There were two quick knocks on the bedroom door, and then another female entered, a much younger Mrs. Ravencroft.

"I came as soon as I heard, Cora." The younger Mrs. Ravencroft sat on the bed, wrapping an arm around Cora to console her. "There, there. Let's not worry until we know what's happened. Have you heard anything?"

Cora removed her hands from her face, and Addison gasped.

It was her—the woman in black.

Mrs. Ravencroft *had* known her.

Struggling to form words, Cora muttered, "No, nothing. Not a word, Catherine."

Catherine. Mrs. Ravencroft's name, the same name as Catherine Earnshaw, the protagonist in *Wuthering Heights*. Catherine's fascination with Emily Bronte made more sense now.

"Raymond has gone out looking for Joseph," Catherine said. "I'm sure he'll find him, and then all this fretting will be for nothing. You'll see. My brother is a skilled sailor. They both are."

"You don't know that. You saw the storm." Cora stared out the window. "I told Joseph not to take the boat out today. I knew it was too windy. He wouldn't listen. He just said he'd been sailing since he was a boy, and I was worrying for nothing."

Catherine walked to the window, her eyes searching the ocean. "Let's not draw any conclusions until we know more. The winds have died down now, and the storm has passed. Maybe he was blown off course and had to find shelter."

Cora shook her head. "I'm afraid, Catherine. Something has happened. I know it has. I don't feel him like I usually do. It's like he's ... like he's—"

"You're not doing yourself or anyone else any favors by losing your mind right now. We're *all* worried. Try to calm down until we know for certain. There's no use getting riled up. Not yet, anyway."

Even in her earlier years, Catherine's pragmatic attitude was apparent. What wasn't certain was the connection between Catherine and Cora.

The sound of a door slamming rattled the house. Cora's eyes widened. She exchanged glances with Catherine, and though Catherine tried to remain calm, her eyes proved she too was on edge.

Heavy footsteps ascended the stairs. A man entered. He was tall, at least six foot five in height, with piercing hazel eyes and a burly physique.

Cora stood, her hands fisted into balls at her sides. "Raymond?"

"What have you learned?" Catherine added.

Raymond glanced at Catherine, then walked over to Cora, clutching her hands in his. He rubbed her palms with his thumbs, stared into her eyes, and said, "I found Joe's boat."

Tears welled in Cora's eyes. "What do you mean you found the boat? What about Joseph? Was he inside? Where is he? Is he all right?"

Raymond paused. "The boat, when I got to it ... it wasn't in good shape. It looked like the sea had destroyed it. It's a miracle I found it at all. The sail was ripped down the middle, and—"

"Raymond," Cora pressed. "I don't care about the boat. *Where* is Joseph?"

Raymond inhaled a long, deep breath of air. "I don't know. I don't ... he wasn't ... he wasn't in the boat when I found it."

Cora's legs collapsed beneath her, her body melting into Raymond's arms.

Raymond looked at Catherine. "I don't think ... she's stopped breathing."

Catherine approached. "Put her on the bed. Let me have a look at her."

Raymond nodded, gently placing Cora's ragdoll body down.

Catherine hung over her, placing a finger beneath Cora's nose. "She's breathing. She's probably just fainted."

"I'll call the doctor."

"Nonsense. She's just had a shock. Give her a moment to recover. She'll be fine."

"I knew I shouldn't have said anything."

"You're right, you shouldn't have. Not the way you said it, anyway. It's your fault, you know. She's under enough stress as it is, with the baby and everything, something you might have considered before opening your mouth." Catherine slapped Cora's cheek. "Come on now, wake up."

Cora's eyes fluttered open. She looked at Catherine. "What happened?"

"You fainted." Catherine turned toward Raymond. "Get her some water, would you?"

He nodded and left the room.

At the same time, Gene entered. He tilted his head, staring at Cora, confused. "How is she?"

"Not well. She's had a shock."

"Is there anything I can do?"

"Unless you know how to mend her broken heart, I should say not."

"I thought he'd be okay," Gene said. "He's used to those waters. We all are."

"He may well be, but the sea was a different animal today."

Glancing over her shoulder, Addison noticed Billy sitting in a chair.

It's not possible. I'm in a memory. How can he be here with me?

"Billy?" Addison asked. "Can you see me?"

He nodded. "You said you'd play with me, and you didn't."

He hopped off of the chair and floated toward the bedroom door. Addison followed after him.

"Wait! Billy, hold on."

He stopped. "Why? You're just like everyone else."

"Did you see who pushed me out of the window earlier?"

He looked down, fiddling with a button on his shirt.

"You did see," Addison said. "Didn't you?"

"I don't want to talk about it."

"Why not?"

"Because the bad person might come."

"Who will come? Who's the bad person? Does the bad person talk to you?"

"No."

"Does the bad person see you?"

"I don't know."

"Whose vision am I in now? Is this *your* vision? Did *you* bring me here?"

Billy lifted a finger and shook his head, pointing at the bed. "*She* did."

"Cora?"

He nodded.

"Do you know why?"

"She wants you to see."

"Why is she still here? Why can't she leave?"

"She's waiting."

"For what?"

"She's afraid the bad person is going to do bad things."

"Who is the bad person, Billy?"

Billy cupped a hand, holding it out to Addison. She looked down. It was then she realized she was still holding the red ball. "I'll toss it back to you and we can keep playing if you tell me about the bad person, okay?"

"I ... I don't know. She said I can't tell you. Not yet."

"How about this—you don't have to say the bad person's name out loud. You can whisper the name into my ear."

Billy shrugged. "And then you'll play with me?"

Addison nodded.

"Oh-kay."

Addison crouched down, but as soon as the ball released from her hands, the room began spinning again. This time when everything came to a stop, she found herself back in the present, in the same room where everything had started. The ball was in the center of the bed. And Billy was gone.

CHAPTER 9

Addison woke a few hours later wrapped in Luke's warm embrace. She rolled over, running a finger along his arm. He yawned, stretching his arms out to the side.

"Where did you run off to last night?" he asked. "I woke up, and you weren't here."

"I couldn't sleep. I went downstairs and ran into Catherine in the parlor."

He raised a brow. "Okay, wait. I'm confused. Who's Catherine?"

"Mrs. Ravencroft."

"Huh. Okay."

"Luke, last night I … no. I need to start from the beginning."

Luke propped a pillow up behind him. "Is this going to be a short story or a long one? Should I grab some coffee first?"

He winked.

Addison frowned.

He reached out, running a hand through Addison's hair. "I'm sorry. I didn't mean to disrespect you. You have my full attention. What's going on?"

"Something bad happened here, Luke. In the manor or outside of it—I'm not sure yet. I'm still trying to figure it all out."

"How do you know? Have you seen something?"

"I've seen a lot, and I know what you're going to say—I should have told you before. And you're right."

"All right. Tell me now."

Addison filled Luke in, sharing every detail of what she had experienced since they arrived at the manor. By the look on his face, it was obvious her omission had pained him.

"Why am I only hearing about this now?" he asked.

"I didn't want to worry you, and I didn't want it to affect our wedding."

"Whether it would have or not, we don't keep things from each other. Ever. You should have told me."

"I know. I'm sorry, Luke. To be honest, I didn't want to deal with it at first. Of all the days for it to happen, it didn't seem fair. It was our wedding day. I didn't want anything to ruin it."

"I guess this means we're not checking out today?"

"I have to convince Catherine to let us stay a bit longer, which won't be easy. She doesn't like me, especially after all that's happened. And she lied to me. She knows Cora, which means she knows what happened to her and why. What I don't understand is why she's denying it."

"You pointed out a dead woman and said you saw her walking around the manor as if she were still alive. Think of it from her perspective. She's spooked, and I'm sure she's questioning who you really are and why you're here."

"She knows why we're here. It's not like I showed up pretending to be someone who was getting married."

He placed a hand over hers. "Think about it, though. She doesn't seem like the kind of woman who believes spirits exist. For all she knows, you got married here to throw her off because you have an ulterior motive to drudge up a past she probably wants to forget. And if you're being honest with yourself, you don't really like her either."

He was right.

She didn't.

And she'd never been any good at faking affection for anyone.

"The question now is: how can I get through to her so she'll open up to me?" Addison asked.

"Why don't you just try talking to her—connecting with her without expectations?"

Addison thought about the conversation she'd had with Catherine the night before. Maybe Luke was right. She had a habit of asking too many questions. "I'll try again."

Luke reached out, grabbing his cell phone from the nightstand.

"What are you doing?" Addison asked.

"I have a new home-renovation job I'm supposed do a walkthrough on later on today. I'm going to call and see if I can push it off another few days."

Addison shook her head. "Don't make any changes on my behalf. You head back. I can handle this. We're supposed to leave on our honeymoon a week from today. Whatever is going on here, it might resolve itself faster if I do this on my own. If I don't, we won't be going anywhere."

Luke shook his head. "I don't like it. I don't feel right about leaving you."

"I won't be alone. I'm sure Gran will stay with me, and nothing is going to happen with her around. Besides, you won't be far. Ocean Beach is only a few hours from Rhinebeck. I'll check in with you throughout the day, and I'll call if anything out of the ordinary happens. I promise."

He pulled her hands up to his lips, kissing them. "I don't know, Addison. I still don't think it's a good idea."

"How about this. Drive home, do your walkthrough, and then check in with me and see how things are going. If you're still worried, you can head back. Besides, I need you to do me a favor."

"Which is?"

"My father doesn't know what's happening. Well, he doesn't know much. I'd like to keep it that way. If he thinks I'm sticking around, he'll assume something's wrong. I'm going to tell him I'm spending some time with Gran before the honeymoon, and she's giving me a ride back to Rhinebeck. That way, he will leave with you."

Luke rubbed his chin, considering her request. "How about a compromise? I'll take your father back, drop him at his house, and check in on my renovation project. But I'm returning tonight."

"You really don't have to—"

"I won't be able to sit at home, knowing you're here. If anything happened, I would be too far away to get here fast enough."

Addison conceded to his request, knowing if she tried to deter him, he wouldn't be swayed. It wasn't worth the debate. "All right. I'll see you later on tonight then."

He wrapped his arms around her. "Be careful, but figure out what's going on here so you can be done with this place. I'd like my wife back sooner than later."

CHAPTER 10

There was a knock at their bedroom door.

"Come in," Addison said.

Whitney entered the room, holding a tray in her hands. "I brought you and your husband breakfast."

"Thank you. I'm starving. What's on the menu today?"

"French toast. I make everything from scratch, even the bread. I hope you like it. There's also some fresh fruit and bacon. And I keep forgetting to ask you what you both like to drink, so I have coffee, tea, and orange juice."

"Sounds wonderful. Luke went to talk to my father. He'll be right back, and then we'll eat."

Whitney nodded, and Addison expected her to leave the room. Instead, she just stood there.

"Is everything all right?" Addison asked.

"Oh, yeah, yeah, everything's fine."

"Thanks again for breakfast. I'll bring the plates to the kitchen when we've finished."

Whitney swatted the air. "Oh, don't bother. I'll come back around in an hour and collect it all. Gives me something to do. I ...

umm … I wanted to tell you … I wasn't completely honest with you before."

"About what?"

"When you asked me about kids. I don't want to bother you, though. We can talk later."

"It's no bother." Addison gestured toward a chair. "Do you want to sit down?"

Whitney glanced to the side, like she expected Catherine to be lurking somewhere close. "I shouldn't, but maybe just for a minute." She sat down, crossing one leg over the other. "When I said I couldn't have kids, I didn't mean to say I was infertile. I meant it's too hard for me to have them."

Too hard was a broad statement, filling Addison's mind with a checklist of various possibilities on the right way to respond. "What's right for one person isn't always right for another. We all have to look out for our needs sometimes."

"It's just … I had a daughter with my ex-husband."

Whitney blurted the words like they had been locked inside a pressure cooker, desperate to get out.

"Oh?"

"She was born with a heart defect. She lived for three weeks. In our pain to try to get past what happened, my ex thought if we had another child, it would make everything better. He coped with the loss of our daughter by acting like she had never been born in the first place, like all we needed was a quick fix, a do-over, and life would be normal again."

"I can't imagine," Addison said. "I'm sorry."

"I'm not. Not for having her, anyway. They were three of the best weeks of my life. I held her in my arms, sang her to sleep, kissed her tiny forehead. I mean, I knew she wasn't going to make it, but just for a few precious moments, I was a mother. I was *her* mother. I could have had other children with him, I suppose, but there was a void in my heart after she was gone. A void that hasn't gone away until recently."

Addison pulled a few sheets of tissue from the canister beside her bed and offered them to her. "I'm glad you told me."

Whitney blotted her tears away. "My life is different now. Colin is so good to me, and the Ravencrofts have been too. Well, I'm closer to Catherine than I am to Gene. He's kind of ..."

Her words trailed off like she'd decided not to finish the sentence, leaving Addison to wonder what she meant to say and how Whitney had managed to pierce Catherine's ice-cold exterior enough to establish a relationship. "Have you worked for Catherine very long?"

"A couple of years now. It's been the best job I've ever had. Over the last year, she has had less guests, but when it's just the four of us, I still cook, and it feels like we're family."

There was another knock on the door, and Colin came in. He glanced at Addison and then at his teary-eyed wife. "Are you all right?"

She nodded. "I'm great. Just a little girl talk."

He smiled. "Sorry to barge in. I just wondered if you wanted to go to town with me. I'm going to look at a foreclosure that just came up, and wondered if you wanted to give your opinion on whether I should buy it or not."

"I can't leave," Whitney said. "Not yet. I need to gather the dishes from breakfast in a little while and do some clean up in the kitchen."

"I can wait. Can I help?"

Whitney nodded and started for the door. "It was nice talking to you, Addison. Hope we get another chance to spend time together before you leave."

"I'll make sure we do."

CHAPTER 11

Addison tapped on Lia's bedroom door. "Hello? Can I come in?"

"It's unlocked," Lia said.

Addison entered to find Lia dressed casually, back in the clothes Lia loved most.

"Sorry I didn't get a chance to talk to you during the reception last night," Addison said.

"No big deal. It was your wedding night. I figured we would catch up today. What's up?"

"A lot, actually."

Addison filled Lia in on recent events.

"Wow," she said when Addison finished. "So ... I guess you'll be sticking around, then, huh?"

"For now. I'm hoping it won't be for long. I was hoping you could do something for me."

Lia smiled. "Sure, name it."

"It would require you to stick around here for one more day."

"Not a problem. You know me: queen workaholic. I have so many unused vacation days they're practically begging me not to come back yet. What do you need?"

"I'm trying to form a relationship with Catherine Ravencroft so she'll allow me to stay here a bit longer. In the meantime, will you find out everything you can about the history of this place? According to Catherine, the manor was built by her grandfather before being passed down to her father, and then to her. I need to know if this is true, and any information you can find on the family."

"You bet. Family, meaning everyone?"

"Everyone who has ever lived here, how they're related to one another, who's still alive, who's dead, how they died, and if any deaths aside from Cora's are suspicious in any way."

Lia pulled her laptop out of her bag and plopped it down on the bed. "All right. I'll start this way, and I can head to town and do more digging if I don't find anything."

"I really appreciate this, Lia."

Addison stepped into the hall, shocked to find Gene hovering outside Lia's bedroom door.

"Gene, what are you doing?"

"You don't need to go to the trouble of digging up the past," he said. "It won't be necessary."

"How do you know what we just—"

He smacked the wall with a hand and grinned. "This is an old house. The walls are thin. You should know that by now."

"Are you saying you heard everything I just said?"

"Just the tail end, the last several seconds or so." He waved a hand to the side, instructing her to join him. "My wife has stepped out for a while, leaving me in charge."

"Leaving you instructions to keep an eye on me, you mean?"

He giggled. "Something like that. We should talk. Follow me."

CHAPTER 12

Gene patted the empty space next to him on the porch swing. Addison sat down. For an older man, Gene was handsome in a sly-fox sort of way. His dark-gray hair was thick and slicked back, and his eyes twinkled whenever he smiled.

Brad stood on a ladder a few feet in front of them, humming while he trimmed hedges that didn't appear to need any trimming. He glanced at Addison and Gene and nodded. "How's everyone doing today?"

"We're fine, Brad," Gene said. "How about yourself?"

"Been a good day so far. And how are those flowers in your room, Mrs. Flynn?"

"Lovely," Addison said.

"Uhh, Brad, can you give Addison and me some time to ourselves?" Gene asked.

"Sure. It's about time for a lunch break anyway."

He stepped down from the ladder, disappearing around the side of the house.

"It seems your visit here has distressed my wife," Gene began.

"I didn't mean to upset her."

"But you have, and you ask a lot of questions, questions best left where they should be—in the past."

"Why all the secrecy over your family's history? I don't understand."

"Why all the questions about a family you're not in? *I* don't understand."

"I'm just curious, that's all."

He interlaced his fingers on his lap. "I was instructed by Catherine to tell you and your party to pack your things and go. The wedding is over. You should get back to your life, and we need to get back to ours."

"I was hoping to stay another day or two."

"You live in Rhinebeck, don't you?"

Addison nodded.

"It's a small population, you know," he said. "Less than eight thousand people. My younger brother lives there. Floyd Ravencroft. Maybe you know him?"

Addison crossed one leg over the other. "I don't."

"Would it surprise you to learn that he knows you?"

She shook her head. "Not really. Luke works on houses all over the area, and his family has lived there for three generations. They seem to know everyone. I've only been there for a few years now."

"I called my brother this morning, and do you know what he told me?"

Addison shrugged.

"There are whispers in the community," he said.

"Whispers about what?"

"A fair, red-haired woman who inherited Grayson Manor a few years back. Some in the community say she claims to be psychic and communicates with the dead."

It was a shocking revelation, one that rattled her. She had always prided herself on keeping a low profile, on not discussing her abilities with anyone she didn't trust. To learn it was common knowledge, whispered about by the locals, made the thought of living there much less appealing.

Addison pulled a hairband off her wrist, twisting her hair into a bun. "It's all right for you to be straightforward. I assume you're referring to me, and I've never claimed any such thing."

"Haven't you? You say you saw Cora outside of this house. You described her to Catherine—what she looked like—what she was wearing the day she died. And before you ask me how I know, I overheard you talking with Catherine in your room yesterday. Cora died in a black dress. She was buried in a white one. Few people know that, and most who do are dead. So tell me, how is it you know things you couldn't know any other way?"

Addison was beginning to see Gene differently. The most cunning of lions held back, lurking in the grass until the perfect time to strike. Was it possible Gene had her fooled? "You seem to be in the habit of listening to conversations that weren't meant for you."

"It's like I said before: the walls in this house are thin. Little gets by me, and I'm not ashamed to admit I hear things now and then."

It almost sounded like a threat.

"Do you believe in spirits, Mr. Ravencroft?"

He leaned back, closed his eyes. "I believe sometimes things happen which can't be explained. Beyond that, I don't know."

"And what about those with psychic abilities?"

He glanced at her with a wry grin. "Oh, I don't know. I've never met one until now."

"Have you ever had an experience you couldn't explain?"

"Once, several years ago."

"Would you tell me about it?"

"I was driving into town, listening to Elvis on the radio. "Love me Tender" was the song. It had been my father's favorite when he was alive. He used to play it every time we were in the car. His funeral had been a few weeks before, and I put it on, I don't know, to honor him, I guess."

"And to remember."

He nodded. "That too. I had a cup of coffee in my hand. I went to take a sip and it smacked against the steering wheel. Next thing I know it's flying out of my hands. Spilled all over me. I was so shocked I almost forgot I was still driving. And that was when ... well, it was when the car filled with the smell of the brand of cigarettes my father used to smoke. Then, I heard his voice. And I don't care what anyone says, it *was* him all right."

"What did he say?"

"He said to keep my eyes on the road. I looked up and saw a little girl no more than five years old running into the street. She was chasing after her dog. He had broken free from his leash. I slammed on the brakes just in time, missing her by a couple of inches."

"Your father saved her life, and yours."

"He sure did. I would have ended up injured, dead, or in prison. Either way, if she would have died, it would have ruined the rest of my life." He paused a moment. "So is what my brother says true? Do you see those who have passed on from this life, or don't you?"

Addison wanted to believe Gene's story, but the softness in his eyes had changed. They were shifty, always darting around, first at the road, then the ocean, then the front door, and then back at the road again. Was his story a fabrication, or was he worried Catherine would return at any moment and see the two of them sitting together on the swing? And given Gene had been tasked with tossing them out: answering his question truthfully was too risky. She needed to stay, at least until Catherine returned, and she needed to believe Gene hadn't heard all of her conversation with Lia.

"I did see a woman outside of my bedroom window, and she was wearing a black dress. Who she is or was, I can't be sure. Just prior to seeing her, I had been looking at the portraits in the parlor.

I suppose it's possible I saw the photo of Cora and then the woman outside and thought they looked the same. Or maybe my eyes deceived me."

He nodded and cocked an eyebrow. "Did they now?"

"As to what your brother thinks about me, when I inherited Grayson Manor, bones were discovered inside and outside of my house. One set turned out to be a woman who had mysteriously vanished after attending a party there in the early 50s. The other belonged to my grandfather, a man I'm glad I never knew. When something like this happens in a small town, people make up what they will to satisfy themselves. I have no control over what rumors are spread about me or my family."

Gene considered her words. "You're being conservative and modest. I don't blame you, I suppose, but I will warn you. The topic of Cora's death is especially disturbing to Catherine, and I'd like to ask you not to discuss it with her again."

"Why not?"

"You have your reasons for the things you do, and I have mine. I'm not going to force you to leave, but once Catherine returns, she will." He gripped the metal bar on the side of the swing, using it as an aid to help him stand up. "And as for your conversation with your friend, you should be careful what you drudge up. The few members of Catherine's family who are still alive won't take kindly if they find out you're poking around. They'll want to know why, and unlike me, they're not as nice."

He tipped his head in Addison's direction, leaving her to contemplate the severity of his words. But she was too busy staring at the way Gene's hands swung as he walked, and thinking how perfectly strong they were for such an old man—just strong enough to shove someone out a second-story window.

CHAPTER 13

Marjorie sat on a chair at a small, two-person table in her bedroom, her eyes focused on the wrapping paper she'd brought with her to wrap Addison's wedding gift in. The paper was decorated with metallic owls in various sizes and shapes, and though the birds had a symbolic meaning, using the paper didn't seem necessary anymore, and Marjorie decided the gift would be best presented as-is.

She grabbed the roll of paper, plopped it into the trash bin, and reached out, grabbing a small leather book off the nightstand. The book was a few inches smaller than a magazine, over three hundred pages, and infinitely more special, because the book wasn't really a book at all—it was a means of attaining a higher power—a power stronger than the mediums in her family possessed on their own.

Marjorie smoothed a hand over the embossed images on the book's cover. Three women clutching one another's hands stood around what appeared to be a cauldron. When viewed more closely, however, what looked to be a cauldron was actually a magnificent pillar of light. And the women surrounding the light—a grandmother, a daughter, and a granddaughter—symbolized the sacred gift they had been born with, a gift passed down from woman to child, generation after generation.

The book had been in Marjorie's possession much longer than intended. She had hoped to pass it down to her own daughter, but when her daughter rejected the gift she was born with, Marjorie was forced to wait for the day Addison stepped up, accepting her duty within the family. When to give the book to Addison had been another matter. Marjorie had considered it after Addison's encounter with Roxanne Rafferty, the woman whose skeleton had been found trapped within the walls of Grayson Manor. But at the time, Addison was just starting to explore her gift, and Marjorie thought it best to wait.

So she did.

The pages of the book contained what appeared to be lines of lyrical poetry, but when spoken by a medium, the words evolved into something much more. Flipping through its sacred pages now, Marjorie was still hesitant about letting the book go. Not because Addison hadn't earned it, and not because it wasn't time, but because she still remembered the day it had been passed to her by her own mother. And though she didn't want to part with it, she knew she had no choice now. She had to. Addison was ready. And even if she wasn't, Marjorie's days were limited. She could feel the life ebbing from her like sand in a sieve. Soon she'd be nothing more than ash, and she would leave this world behind.

CHAPTER 14

Addison walked downstairs, pausing halfway when she heard a man and woman engaged in a heated conversation. The woman's voice was Catherine's, but the man's was one she'd never heard before. Craning her head, she had a two-inch view inside Catherine's bedroom, which offered her a glimpse of the man's side profile. He was older and tall, Catherine's age perhaps, and wearing a gray ascot cap over his bald head.

"I don't care what you think," Catherine said. "It's not up to you."

"It should be," the man replied.

"Well, it isn't."

"I won't let you do it."

"You won't *let me*? I don't know what power you think you have, but you don't have any. If you've said what you wanted to say, I want you out of my house. Leave. Now."

"Out of *our* house, you mean."

"This place was never yours."

"I'm not going anywhere until we've worked this out."

Catherine snorted a laugh. "There's nothing to work out. And if you think you can show up here and bully—"

Catherine stopped midsentence.

"What is it?" the man asked. "What kind of game are you playing?"

"Shh!"

"Why?"

"Someone outside, on the stairway, listening."

Addison rushed downstairs, rounded the corner, and stood, her heart racing, her hand clasped over her mouth.

Catherine stepped into the hall. "Who's there?"

The man stepped out behind her. "No one is out here. You're either being paranoid or playing games. We're not finished talking."

"We're finished talking when I say we are."

Addison heard Catherine's bedroom door slam shut. The man cleared his throat. It sounded like he was in the hallway, and Catherine had shut him out.

The conversation, it seemed, was over.

CHAPTER 15

I found something," Lia said. "It isn't much, but it's a start. The newspaper has a searchable archive. Here's what I found for Joseph."

Lia turned her laptop toward Addison. The article was dated June 17, 1964.

Local Sailor Still Missing

Tragedy struck close to home when Joseph Blackthorn, a twenty-two-year old experienced sailor went missing five days ago while aboard his boat, Cora's Heart. *The vessel disappeared several miles from shore after heading into one of this season's most brutal storms. Debris from Blackthorn's demolished boat has been found scattered across the ocean's surface, but as of this time, Joseph has not been located.*

Search crews have scoured the wreckage site over the last several days, but so far there has been no sign of the missing sailor. Despite numerous pleas made by Joseph's wife, Cora, to continue looking for her husband, local police believe it's likely Blackthorn drowned after his boat capsized during the storm, and any future attempts to locate him have been called off.

Joseph is survived by his wife, Cora, and several members of the Blackthorn family, who are also residents of Ocean Beach. Funeral arrangements are being made for next Tuesday, with services held at the Holy Trinity Church at two o'clock in the afternoon.

"I also found a short obituary for Cora," Lia said, "and another for William Ravencroft. He was six when he died, and aside from the fact he died so young, there's another, even more unusual part of the story."

Addison raised a brow. "What did you find out?"

Lia typed a few words on her computer and turned the screen back to Addison. "Cora and Billy died on the same day."

CHAPTER 16

Addison waved to Luke and her father, watching them back out of the driveway and head down the road. Seeing them go was bittersweet, but something she had to do. Lia offered to do more digging on the Blackthorn family's history, but Addison asked her to hold off. She needed to talk to Catherine first.

Addison walked back inside the manor to find Catherine waiting in the entryway, tapping the bottom of her ballet flat on the wood floor like a restless mother anxious to scold her child.

"Your husband just left," Catherine said. "Why didn't you leave with him?"

"I'd like to stay a bit longer if it's all right. Just another couple of days or so. I'll pay you double the room rate."

Catherine glanced at her watch. "One hour, twenty-seven minutes."

Addison leaned against the wall, crossing a leg in front of her. "Excuse me?"

"One hour, twenty-seven minutes. That's how long you have until checkout, and that's how long you have to leave. I hope your grandmother is prepared to drive you home."

"Can we talk?"

"We just did."

"Not about when you want me to leave, about why I want to stay."

"I don't care why you want to stay. You can't."

"Why not?" Addison asked.

"I have more guests arriving. I'll need your room."

It was a lie. Earlier, when Catherine was gone, Addison had snuck into Catherine's office, checking the reservation book. There were no future bookings, not a single one.

"I know we got off to a rocky start," Addison said. "I was hoping we could try again."

"Whatever for? There's no need. We're not going to be friends. We're not even going to be acquaintances."

"If you would just hear me—"

Catherine squinted. "You're not as smart as you think you are, you know. I see what you're doing here."

"I'm not *doing* anything. I don't get to spend much time with my gran nowadays, and I thought it would be nice to spend an extra day or two with her before we head back home."

"So now you expect me to allow your grandmother to stay here longer too."

Addison nodded. "Yes, I was hoping we both could. My friend Lia would like to tag along too."

Catherine glanced back at her watch. "One hour, twenty-one minutes, and then I'll expect you all to be out. Whitney informed me she took breakfast to your room some time ago. You've been fed. I suggest you start packing."

Catherine whirled around and walked down the hall.

"Wait," Addison said. "Please. Just give me one minute."

"I just gave you six. I don't have time for more. Even if I did, I wouldn't spend them with you."

Catherine rounded the corner, leaving Addison with a decision —take a gamble she didn't want to take or find another way. When no alternatives came to mind, she went after Catherine, catching up with her in the kitchen. "I … ahh … found something in my room, and I wanted to give it to you."

Without looking her direction, Catherine pulled several plates out of the dishwasher and deposited them on the shelf. "What do you mean—you *found* something?"

Addison removed the red ball from her sweater pocket, bouncing it on the ground. Once, twice, and then a third time, until it achieved the desired result. Catherine's eyes widened like saucers. She lunged at Addison, snatching the ball out of her hand. She stared at it for a time like she couldn't believe what she was seeing, turning the ball over inside her palm until she noticed a tiny divot in the side—a divot she seemed to recognize. "I haven't seen this in so many … I can't believe … it's not possible … there's no way … I've searched for this for so … there's no way it could show up after all this …"

"Allow me to explain."

Catherine squeezed the ball in her hand. "You've been snooping again. Where did you find this? The truth this time."

"*He* gave it to me."

"*He* … who?"

Addison stared at Catherine and whispered, "Your son—Billy."

CHAPTER 17

Catherine pressed a hand to her chest like she was struggling for breath. "How can you be so cruel? Why would you say something like that?"

"If you could just hear me out," Addison said. "I'll explain everything."

Catherine stumbled to the kitchen table and sat down, her eyes focused on Billy's ball clenched in her hand.

Addison sat across from her.

"How do you know about my son?" Catherine asked. "Did Gene tell you? He must have told you. He's always taking too many liberties with our guests."

It was a loaded question, a ticking time bomb with no right answer. Whether she told the truth or whether she lied, it wouldn't make much of a difference. Catherine would either believe her, or she wouldn't, and odds favored the latter. "It wasn't Gene."

"Whitney then?"

Addison shook her head. "Do you know what a psychic medium is?"

"I'm familiar with the term, but you're avoiding my question."

"I am a medium. I have the ability to communicate with spirits at times, with those who have passed on from this life. I can see and experience things from the past, present, or future, depending on the situation."

Addison went silent, letting her words hang in the air while she evaluated Catherine's reaction. She expected Catherine to lash out in a furious tirade, but Catherine remained stolid, her expression blank.

"You don't know me," Addison said, "so I know how hard it must be for you to believe what I'm saying is true. I am telling the truth, though."

Catherine waved a hand in the air. "I'm guessing there's a point to all of this. Get to it."

Addison leaned back in the chair. "I … ahh … I never know when I'm going to be contacted by a spirit. Sometimes I go months without a visitation. Other times it's a matter of days. When contact *is* made I don't always know what they want or why they've reached out, but there's always a reason, something they want or need to happen, even though sometimes they themselves don't always know what it is."

"Why you? What could you possibly do to help? They're dead. What more do they need?"

"They're trapped here, between this life and the next. Some don't know how to move on. Others can't move on. It's my job to figure out why they're still here and what they need in order to enter the afterlife."

Catherine rapped her fingernails along the table's surface. "I was raised to believe life exists after this one, that there's something waiting for us all, something to make the hell we endure in this life worth it in the end. I've always imagined at the moment of death, a person's soul is swept away, taken to a better place. If true, why wouldn't it be the same for everyone? Why would some leave and others stay? Why would anyone be *trapped* here?"

"Most people do move on. In my experience, those who don't usually suffered a traumatic event just prior to their death. Some seem tortured, unaware of how they died or what needs to happen in order for them to move on. Others cling to this life and refuse to leave. That's where I come in."

Catherine's demeanor softened, but Addison didn't believe her words had swayed her. The ball had conjured tender memories Catherine had stowed so deep inside herself, she'd forgotten what it was like to feel them anymore. It made sense now. Catherine's tough, rigid exterior was partially a façade, a front she displayed to others in order to mask her pain.

The death of a son.

Catherine's *only* son.

It was the kind of grief Addison couldn't imagine.

Still, there were questions.

Why had Billy died so young?

What had happened to the boy?

The sound of wind chimes dancing into each other outside the kitchen window brought Catherine back to herself again. "How is it you claim to possess such a gift?"

"It is passed down through the women in my family and has been for several generations."

"So your grandmother, Marjorie. She fancies herself a medium too?"

Addison nodded.

"You're crazy," Catherine said. "You do know that, don't you?"

"I understand how it must seem to you. One day I was a normal child, and the next I picked an innocent-looking penny off the sidewalk and saw a homeless man's future."

Catherine smacked a hand on the table, tossed her head back, and laughed. "Well, I'll give you this. I haven't been this amused in a long time. I don't know what you think you know about my son, or what you think you've seen, but I don't believe in ghosts, and I don't believe in psychic abilities, either. Dead is dead. Spirits don't come back, no matter how much you want them to."

"I used to feel the same way. I didn't want any part of what I'd inherited at first. It didn't seem fair that people I had never met before could enter my life, needing my help. In ways it made me angry. I'm expected to help perfect strangers, and yet I lack the ability to communicate with my own mother."

Catherine raised a brow. "When your family arrived, I wondered why she wasn't with them. Since you seem so keen on sharing stories, you won't mind telling me what happened to her, yes?"

"She died in a car accident five years ago."

"Yes, well, I can see how it would be a tragic thing for you to go through. Here one minute, gone the next. It's the hardest way to lose someone, in my opinion. You never quite get past it. It's the one thing that sticks with you over time and never goes away."

"No, it doesn't."

"I will say one thing. In talking to you now, I can tell how passionate you are about this psychic-ability business. And though I don't share your beliefs, I believe you actually think you possess such a power."

Addison considered Catherine's statement to be a move in a positive direction. She didn't need Catherine to believe her as much as she needed Catherine to see her as someone who wasn't out to do her harm. "If you don't mind, I would like to know more about the manor."

Deep in thought, Catherine glanced around the room. "The estate holds many memories for me. Some of them good. Some bad. My grandfather built it when I was a child. He wasn't the nicest person. Actually, *nice* isn't a word I'd use to describe him at all. He tormented us as children. We were all terrified of him. Whenever we heard him coming, we'd all run and hide."

"What happened to him?"

"Eventually he did us all a favor by drinking himself to death. It's strange, you know? I still feel him sometimes, like he's still here in this house, watching my every move, judging me, even though I'm smart enough to know it isn't true. It's funny how the negativity of a single, ignorant person has had the power to plague me throughout my life, even when I knew what he thought of me wasn't true. It's like an axe, I suppose, slowly chipping away at me until there was nothing left to chip."

Did the spirit of Catherine's grandfather, or even her father— still reside within these walls?

And was one of them the spirit that Billy feared?

"I'm sorry."

"I'm not," Catherine said. "Life isn't about being happy. It's about enduring what comes your way and learning to live with it. We're all survivors in our own way."

"I assume your father left you the manor when he died?"

Catherine nodded. "Not because he wanted it to go to me. He didn't. He made his decision out of spite. It should have passed to my brother Raymond, but my father made sure it didn't."

"Why?"

"He wanted to teach Raymond a lesson, and he succeeded."

"What did Raymond do to upset your father?"

"He went against my father's wishes. It was a long time ago, and it doesn't matter now. I took it over, even though I would have had a better life if I had left this place." Setting the ball on the table, she said, "You could have just told me where you found this instead of making up a story to get me to talk about my son."

Just when Addison thought they'd reached square two, she was dropped back to one.

"I understand you don't believe me, but I didn't make it up. I haven't lied to you about anything."

"If you expect me to believe you have magical powers, you'll have to prove it. Otherwise, I think we've bonded enough for one lifetime."

"How do you expect me to prove it to you?"

Catherine shrugged. "What about a demonstration? You say you've communicated with my son. Summon Billy. Right here, right now. Bring him back to me."

"I can't give you what you want. I wish I could. It's true: I have seen him in this house, but only once."

"Where?"

"In a bedroom upstairs, the one a few doors down from mine. I believe it was his when he was alive."

"And when did this alleged vision of yours take place?"

"Right after we talked in the parlor last night."

"My son was the sweetest boy. A good boy. Why would he be trapped here? Why wouldn't he be able to move on?"

"I don't know. He hasn't told me yet."

"What *has* he told you?"

"The important thing is, I believe he's waiting for something to happen first."

"Like what?"

Addison shrugged. "He seems to think he's leaving here soon. When I asked him where he was going, he said he was going away, but he didn't say where. And there's something else ..."

"Something like what?"

"He's afraid of someone he calls 'the bad person.' I have tried to get him to give me more information, but he wouldn't."

"*Useless*," Catherine said. "I don't know why I'm still sitting here with you. You're spinning stories, 'going around the houses,' as they say. Nothing you say leads anywhere. It just loops around and doesn't make sense."

She scooted the chair back.

"Even if I could get Billy to appear right now, you wouldn't be

71

able to see him," Addison said. "I'm the only one who can, and that only happens when he allows it."

"I knew it." Catherine rolled the ball toward Addison. "I don't know where this toy came from, but it didn't belong to my son. So take it. Take it back, and get out of my house."

"You know it's his. I can tell."

Addison reached out and grabbed it. When she returned her attention to Catherine, Billy was standing beside her, his hand resting on his mother's shoulder.

"Are you deaf?" Catherine asked. "I just told you to get out of my house. And yet, for whatever reason, you're still sitting there, staring at me like I have pie all over my face."

Billy waved at Addison.

Not wanting to alarm Catherine any further, Addison only smiled back.

Billy looked at his mother. "I'm sorry, Mama. I know I wasn't supposed to go past the gate."

He turned toward Addison and nodded.

"Billy is sorry he went past the gate," Addison said. "Does that mean anything to you?"

Catherine's eyes widened, her face a combination of pain and disbelief. "The gate? There's no way ... how could you possibly ... you're saying *he* told you this? He told you this himself?"

Addison nodded, assuming Billy's comment had something to do with the day he died. "Do you know what he means?"

"He wasn't allowed to go past the gate—not alone—not unless Gene or I were there with him."

"What happened?"

She closed her eyes like she was picturing it in her mind. "One minute he was right there, standing next to me. I had a basket of sheets and was hanging them on the line. He started tugging on my dress. He wanted me to play with him. I shooed him away, said I was busy. I had chores to do. We would play later. The wind kicked up. I glanced down where he had been standing and noticed he wasn't there anymore."

Had Billy slipped past his mother, deciding to play in the ocean, and drowned? If Addison's hunch was right, it explained why he'd been stuck in between this life and the next for so long. Had the sea taken him like it took Joseph? Had his body never been found?

It all seemed logical until Billy shook his head.

Was it possible?

Could he understand her thoughts without any words being spoken between them?

Without speaking, she looked at him.

Can you hear me? Can you hear my thoughts?

Billy nodded.

Did you die in the ocean?

He shook his head.

Did you die because you went past the gate?

He nodded.

What happened to you?

"I wanted to know where she was going," he said.

Where who was going? Your mother?

He shook his head. "My auntie."

Cora?

He nodded. "I saw her crying. She was sad. She was always sad, and I wanted to make her feel better."

Addison pressed a hand to her mouth.

"What's going on with you?" Catherine asked. "Hello? You're not talking now?"

"I know what happened," Addison said, "the day Billy died. I know why he went past the gate."

Catherine rolled her eyes. "Oh, stop. You don't know anything."

Addison stood, placed her hands on her hips. "He was following Cora."

Catherine shot out of her seat, her eyes narrow like a cat ready to strike. Voice raised, she said, "Never speak her name in front of me again! Do you hear me?"

"Why not? What happened that day? Catherine, please. Tell me. Did he die trying to save her?"

Catherine covered her face with her hands.

A tear rolled down Billy's cheek. "I don't want to be dead."

I'm so sorry, Billy. You need to go home.

"I am home."

You need to go to the place everyone else goes when they pass on.

"I can't, not without my mama!"

In an instant, Billy was gone.

"Help me help your son, Catherine," Addison said. "Help me help you."

"You can't. There's nothing you can do for me, and there's nothing you can do for him. He's dead, and it's all her fault. *She's* the one who killed him."

CHAPTER 18

Addison wadded up her clothes, tossing them into the suitcase like they were live grenades. "I don't know what more I can do now, Gran. At this point I'm sure we've been thrown out. We have to leave."

Marjorie shook her head. "I warned you not to push."

"I didn't have a choice. I thought I was getting through to her. It seemed like she actually started to believe me. Her voice changed, her demeanor softened. For a moment I had her believing *what if –* what if there was a chance I was telling the truth? And then I mentioned Billy, and I realized I'd pushed too far. I've lost my focus. I don't know what more to do at this point."

Gran pushed the suitcase to the side. "Come here. Sit beside me for a few minutes."

"I can't. I'm too wound up. There's no possible way I can relax right now. Besides, we're supposed to be leaving."

"I need you to trust me. Can you?"

Addison sighed, then nodded.

"Then do what I ask," Marjorie said.

Addison joined her on the bed. "All right, now what?"

"I have something for you. I thought about offering it as a wedding gift. I was even going to wrap it. But it's more than a gift. Much more. And it isn't for Luke. It's for you."

"Oh … kay. Where is it?"

Marjorie reached into her handbag and pulled out the book. "Here."

Though Marjorie had pushed it in Addison's direction, Addison thought it odd that when she reached out to take it, Marjorie didn't release it to her right away. Instead, she clutched it tightly and didn't let go.

"Are you just wanting me to look at it, or are you giving it to me?" Addison asked.

Marjorie lifted her hand off the book. "I … yes. It's yours now."

Addison studied the book's cover and was reminded of a time when she was a little girl. She'd entered her mother's room and saw her writing in a leather book similar to this one. When she had asked her mother what it was, her mother said it was a journal, just a place she kept her thoughts. "Is this my mother's journal?"

Marjorie shook her head. "This book never belonged to your mother. It should have, but she was unwilling to accept it. I held on to it, hoping one day I would leave it to you, and now the time has come for you to have it."

Marjorie's tone was heavy, her words serious in nature. And though Addison wanted to open the book, she held back. "What is it?"

"Our history. Think of it as an addition."

"An addition to what?"

"To the powers you already possess."

"There's more?" Addison asked.

"Much more. The book will explain everything."

"Why did you wait so long to give it to me?"

"I wanted to be sure you were ready. You understand, don't you?"

Addison didn't understand. She'd never felt ready to accept what she was—not the first time her abilities had manifested as a child, and not now. It didn't seem like there was a right time or a wrong time to have been given the book. Marjorie had withheld it from her, causing Addison to wonder what else she'd been hiding. Marjorie hadn't seemed like herself lately. She'd been quieter, more introspective, a far cry from the feisty woman who never missed an opportunity to speak her mind.

"What else haven't you told me?" Addison asked.

"Nothing. This is it."

"It isn't though. I can feel it. You know I can. You're not telling me something."

Marjorie tapped her fingernail on the book. "With this book, you'll have all the power you can possess, everything I have."

"I'm not talking about the book. I'm talking about you. You haven't been yourself since you arrived here."

"Let's focus on this right now. One thing at a time. I know it isn't the answer you want, but it's the only answer you're getting today. Now, instead of fearing the power you hold in your hands, embrace it. Take a look inside."

Frustrated and left with unanswered questions, Addison scanned the book's cover. "What is this?" Addison asked. "A book of spells?"

Marjorie laughed. "Of course not. We're *not* witches. Look closer. What do you see?"

"Women standing around a ..."

"Pillar of light. The light is a symbol of our gifts—the gifts passed from grandmother, to mother, to child over time."

Addison peeled the book cover back, scanning the first few pages. The written verses were short—most only a few lines. They had been penned in cursive in black ink. Some were delicate and fluid. Others were like chicken scratches—craggy and hard to read.

Each verse within the book offered guidance; each page was marked with a burgundy-wax seal pressed into the paper, much like the nobles had used to secure private, royal documents. The seal matched the emblem on the book's cover of three women huddled in what Addison perceived to be a spiritual embrace. Beneath each seal was a date, the earliest being 1619.

Marjorie reached out, snapping the book shut. "You can look through the rest later."

"If they're not spells, what are they, then?"

"A bit of extra help only to be used when necessary."

"If they help, why not use them all the time?"

"When spoken aloud, these verses call upon the spirits of your female ancestors, those who lived before you, doing what you do now."

"Are you saying they will appear to me?"

"I'm saying they will hear you, and they have the temporary ability to guide you in ways you can't always guide yourself."

Marjorie set the book beside her on the bed and leafed through part of it, pausing when she seemed to have found the page she wanted. "Do you want to know how it works?"

Addison nodded.

Marjorie turned her palms up. "Give me your hands."

CHAPTER 19

Addison placed her palms on top of her grandmother's. In the past, when joined hands, it had always resulted in conjuring a spirit, at times forcing an entity to appear whether they wanted to or not.

"Okay, I want you to close your eyes and breathe," Marjorie said.

Addison did as instructed.

"Now, inhale all the air you can fill inside of your lungs. Hold it for as long as you can, and when you can't hold it any longer, breathe it all the way out. Relax your body. Clear your mind. When your mind is clear, you will see what you need to see."

"How long do I need to—"

"Shhh. You'll know when the time is right. You'll know when you're ready."

Ready for what?

Relaxing seemed impossible right now.

Her breath was shallow and tight, her lungs feeling like they were on the verge of collapse. And nothing was happening.

"Concentrate, Addison," Marjorie said. "Focus on your breath."

If only it were that easy.

Relax.

Quiet my mind.

Breathe positivity in.

Push negativity out.

She repeated the silent affirmations in her mind until she felt herself let go, becoming still, hearing only the sound of her grandmother's voice:

Ancient mothers far and near

Heed my voice, lend an ear

With these wings allow her flight

Protection and the gift of sight

Her eyes opened.

She was no longer with her grandmother in the bedroom.

She was outside, perched on a branch in a tree.

The sun's beamed down, warming her face. She tried pressing a hand to her cheek, but she didn't feel skin. She felt something else, something much softer—feathers. She looked down, noticed she'd transformed into a magnificent owl.

An old woman sat next to her, dressed in a dress so white she appeared to be glowing.

"Who are you?" Addison asked.

The woman smiled. "Listen and see."

Through the wind, she heard her grandmother's voice.

Flap your wings and fly, Addison.

Let them take you where you're meant to go.

See what you're meant to see.

Addison leapt off the branch, soaring across the ocean, farther and farther until all that existed was the open sea. In the distance, she spotted a sailboat. It was small and white, thrashing back and forth atop a furious, turbulent sea. Water spit from the ocean's surface, drenching the boat then sliding back into the ocean again. Addison swooped down, her talons gripping the bow's railing.

Drenched and worn, a man fought against the sea's rage, his hands clasping a rope, pulling himself toward the sail.

Joseph.

Fighting a raging sea, Joseph inched closer to the sail, only to reach it, look up, and discover it was ripped, torn beyond repair.

He slapped a hand over his eyes, shouting, "No, no, no!"

A monstrous wave rose up, crashing onto the deck. This time, the sea wasn't as forgiving. Joseph catapulted into the air, shooting straight up before plunging into the ocean below. Addison's eyes darted around, searching the water, watching for any sign of him. Seconds passed, then minutes. The boat capsized, dumping the water from the deck back into the sea. The scene blurred together like hours passing in seconds. When it came back into focus again, the sea was quiet and serene as if nothing had happened here.

The boat floated in pieces on the water's surface. Not far from the wreckage, Addison noticed something else bobbing at the water's surface. She swooped down to get a closer look.

It couldn't be.

But it was.

Joseph!

Weak and frail, somehow he had survived long enough to wrap his body around a piece of floating debris. His body showed no movement, no signs of life. His chest was bare now with the exception of a brown braided necklace clinging to his neck. Dangling from the center was a small, silver cross.

Addison stared at him, gasping when his eyes flashed open. His breath was shallow, but still there.

He was alive!

In the distance, a slow hum grew to a loud vibration. Another boat was on the water, moving in Joseph's direction. If Joseph heard it, he gave no indication. His eyes closed again, and he mumbled, "I'm sorry, Cora. I tried to make it back to you. I'm sorry."

CHERYL BRADSHAW

"No, Joseph!" Addison shouted. "Not now. Not when you've fought so hard. Just a little longer. Please. Help is on the way. It's your brother, Raymond. I'm sure of it. He's coming for you. He's almost here."

But her words were meaningless, unable to alter the past.

There was nothing to be done.

No way to reshape history now.

Joseph's arms went limp, causing his entire body to slip beneath the water. The piece of debris he'd been clutching drifted away. Addison watched in horror as Joseph's body sank into the ocean until he faded from sight.

"I'm sorry, Joseph," Addison whispered. "So sorry I couldn't help you."

A gust of wind surged like a tornado, circling around her, forcing her toward shore. She was back at the manor again, but given its pristine condition, it wasn't the present. A much younger-looking Catherine stood in the front yard, pinning sheets on a clothesline while a Patti Page song played on the radio. Billy weaved around his mother, playing peek-a-boo, hiding behind the clothes and springing out when she least expected it.

Catherine reached out and patted him on the head. "You silly boy."

"When are you going to play with me, Mama?"

"Later. After the chores are done."

Billy hung his head. "Aww. You said that yesterday, and then you never did."

"Yesterday I had to go into town. I'm sorry things don't always turn out the way you expect them to, son. That's life. When you're older, you'll understand. Why don't you run inside and find the new ball I bought you?"

He crossed his arms in front of his chest and huffed. "No, I don't want to."

"Why not?"

82

"I just don't."

Billy flopped to the ground, yanking blades of grass through his fingers.

Catherine looked at him and frowned. "Billy, I'll tell you what. When I'm done hanging these clothes, I'll play with you. My other chores can wait."

Billy shrugged. "You mean it?"

"I promise."

Catherine smiled down at her son, and for the first time, Addison witnessed a period in Catherine's life when she was full of joy. Gone was the stern, hard exterior. She was soft; her eyes, kind.

A few minutes later as Catherine shifted her focus back to hanging the last two sheets, the manor's front door opened and Cora stepped out wearing the all-too-familiar black dress. Cora's eyes were puffy and swollen, her face a picture of despair. Busy clipping the last sheet to the line, Catherine didn't notice Cora walk past the gate, or Billy run out of the manor, following her. Addison spread her wings and flew ahead, certain where Cora was going—to the lookout point.

She was right.

Once there, Cora gazed out to sea and said, "I've tried, Joseph. I really have. I've tried living without you all this time, and I can't do it any longer. I just can't. I don't want to be in this world if you're not in it with me. I feel alone without you. I'm lost, and tired. So tired. Forgive me."

As Cora's body teetered over the edge, a frightened, confused Billy rushed to her side. "Auntie, Auntie, stop. No!"

He reached his tiny hand out, grappling for the fabric on her dress. It slipped through his fingers. He jumped forward, trying again, this time clutching a handful of the dress in his hands just as she went over. Cora shouted Joseph's name and plummeted to the shore below, taking Billy with her.

Billy screamed, and within seconds, Catherine's voice howled through the air like a wolf communicating with her pack. "Billy? Billy, where are you?"

Addison turned, her eyes surveying the area until Catherine came into view. Hand cupped over her forehead like a visor, Catherine ran past the open gate and hurried along the shore, her head twisting in all directions, searching for the one thing Addison wished she never had to find. She neared the point Billy and Cora had stood moments before and called out to him again.

At first, looking over the edge didn't seem to occur to her. Then her eyes came to rest on Billy's red ball. It had fallen from his hands, lodging inside the crevice of a rock. Catherine squinted, reached down, and picked it up. Puzzled, she rolled it around the palm of her hand.

The grisly truth didn't take long, the harsh reality consuming her until her face was covered in tears. She hadn't even discovered his body, and yet, somehow she knew.

She stepped up to the ledge and looked down, the red ball slipping through her fingers as she screamed into her hands.

Addison turned away.

I've seen enough.

I don't want to be in this memory.

I don't want to be here anymore.

She squeezed her eyes shut and then opened them again, forcing herself out of the nightmare and into the light.

She was back in the room again, her grandmother sitting in front of her.

"What did you see?" Marjorie asked.

Everything.

I saw everything.

Things I needed to see, but wished I hadn't.

"It was horrible, Gran. So much pain has happened here. So much suffering."

She turned toward the door, sensing a presence on the opposite side.

"What is it?" Marjorie asked.

"It's ... Billy. Something's wrong. I can feel it."

Addison rushed to the door, flinging it open to find Billy standing on the other side, trembling.

"What's wrong, Billy?" Addison asked. "Why are you here? What did you come to tell me?"

"Mama needs you. Mama needs you now."

CHAPTER 20

A woman's raucous, blood-curdling shriek ripped through every room and corridor. Addison and Marjorie hastened out of the room, chasing the cry for help to Catherine's door.

Addison jiggled the handle. "It's locked."

"We have to get in there!" Marjorie replied. "Now."

"Catherine! Are you in there? Are you okay?"

A slow, steady moan was heard on the opposite side of the door, followed by a man's voice. It was low and muffled, too hard to make out.

"Gene, is that you?" Addison asked. "What's going on in there?"

Marjorie leaned in, inspecting the door. "It's a regular lock, not a deadbolt. Go to the kitchen. Get me a butter knife."

Addison ran downstairs, riffling through the drawers until she found what she needed. She raced back to the door, placing the knife into Marjorie's hand. Marjorie jammed it inside the crack, forcing the latch back until the door sprung open.

Sprawled on the floor was Catherine, her sweater wet, saturated with blood.

Gene knelt over her, sobbing. "No, no, no. It's going to be all right. You're going to be okay. Don't leave me, Catherine. Please, don't leave me."

Addison's eyes darted around the room, searching for a weapon, anything to explain what had happened.

Addison dropped to the floor next to Gene, pressing her fingers against Catherine's neck. The pulse was faint, but it was there.

Addison took out her cell phone. "I'll call for an ambulance. Gran, find Lia. Bring her here right away."

"Any idea where she is?"

"She said she was going for a walk on the beach before she headed home."

Marjorie nodded and left the room.

Addison made the call, her frustration mounting when the operator pressed for details she couldn't provide. She offered a rapid explanation of the situation and then finished by saying, "I'm sorry, I can't waste time on the phone with you. Just send someone out to the estate as fast as you can. Whatever happened here, I don't believe it was an accident."

Addison shoved the phone back into her pocket.

Lia rushed into the room, kneeling down next to Addison.

"What the hell happened?" Lia asked.

"We don't know yet."

Lia thumbed in Gene's direction. "What did *he* say happened?"

Addison shrugged. "He isn't talking. Not to me, anyway."

Lia leaned over Catherine's body. "All right. I'll have a look."

Addison placed a hand on Gene's shoulder. "Gene, can you back up and give Lia some space?"

He furrowed his brow. "Why? What can she do?"

"*She* can do a lot," Lia replied. "I'm a medical examiner. Now move so I can see if there's anything I can do to help her."

He nodded and inched away, but kept hold of Catherine's hand.

Addison exchanged glances with Marjorie, and Marjorie closed the bedroom door, pressing her back against it. Until they were sure what role Gene had played in this, he wasn't going anywhere.

Lia bent over Catherine and peeled back her shirt, using her fingers to feel around. Locating the source of the bleeding, she pressed down, applying pressure. "Chest wound looks like. There's frothy blood around it."

"From what?"

"Bubbles of blood, caused by air going in and out. Elastic tissue. Gaping. You find a weapon?"

"Not yet."

"She has a bluish tint to her lips. Looks like she may have been stabbed with a sharp object, a knife possibly. We need to seal the wound and stop the air from entering her chest. I don't want her lung to collapse."

Addison nodded. "Okay, what do you need?"

"Plastic. Gauze if you can find it. And tape to seal it up. I'll take whatever we've got. We may be able to stop the bleeding before the medics get here, if we hurry."

Gene headed for the door. "I'll go."

In unison, Addison and Marjorie said, "No!"

"Look," Lia said, "he knows where everything is. We're racing against the clock here."

"I'll go with him." Marjorie said.

"Fine," Lia said. "Just … hurry."

Marjorie and Gene left the room. Once they were out of earshot, Lia turned to Addison. "If you want my honest opinion, I don't think she's going to make it."

"Is there nothing you can do to save her?"

"She's lost a lot of blood, Addison. Her breathing is getting weaker by the second. I don't think we'll be able to save her before the medics—"

Catherine's eyes fluttered open. She reached for Addison and muttered, "You were right. Everything you said. I can see it now. I … I …"

"What happened?" Addison asked. "Who did this to you, Catherine?"

"My darling boy. Oh, how nice it is to see him at last. He's beautiful, you know, just like I remember. Looks just like his father. Always looked like his father. Such a good, strapping young boy. The best boy. He came for me just like I always knew he would one day."

"You see Billy?" Addison asked. "You see him now?"

Catherine raised a finger, pointing.

Addison glanced over her shoulder. A white lace curtain flapped in the breeze in front of an open window. Billy stood beside it. If Catherine could see him, Lia was right. Catherine was dying.

Billy smiled at Addison. "I get to leave now. I get to go to the place Mama always told me about."

"No, Billy," Addison said. "Your mother needs to stay here. I know how much you want to be with her, but if we can keep her alive just a little longer, we can save her."

He shook his head.

"Listen to me!" Addison pleaded. "Can you wait for your mother just a little bit longer?"

Billy stretched a hand toward Catherine. "Come on, Mama. It's okay. We can play now."

Catherine looked at Addison. "You have to let me go. This is what I want. It's what I've always wanted—to be with my boy again."

"Tell me what happened to you, Catherine. Who did this?"

"Leave this place. Today. Take your grandmother and your friend and go away from this house. Forget what has happened here."

"Why?"

"I did something wrong, a long time ago, something I should not have done, and now … now … I'm paying the price for my mistake."

"What mistake?"

"Gene needs to ... you have to help ... you need to ... the police."

"I don't understand," Addison said.

"You're in danger. You're all ... all of you ... in danger. And Gene ..."

Catherine's eyes closed, her head sagging to the side.

Addison looked at Lia. "Is she ..."

Lia felt for a pulse and nodded. "I'm sorry, Addison. She's dead."

CHAPTER 21

Gene and Marjorie returned, the items he'd rushed to gather spilling from his hands the moment he saw Catherine's lifeless body.

"I'm sorry, Gene," Lia said.

"Sorry? Oh, no. No, no, no. Is she … dead?"

"She lost too much blood. There was nothing we could do for her."

Gene sank to the floor. He bent his knees toward his chest, burrowing his head inside, sobbing. Seeing him in this feeble, demoralized state made it far too easy for Addison to make assumptions—far too easy to lie to herself, to believe what was before her—a broken, grieving man—a man, chanting to himself about not being able to survive this life without his "darling Cat."

Whether it was a spectacular display of sorrow or an elaborate hypocrisy remained to be seen. No matter what Addison believed, Gene had been the only one in the room with Catherine when she arrived, and aside from the bedroom door, there was only one other way out—the window, which was open.

Curious.

In order to entertain the idea that Catherine's murderer wasn't Gene and the actual killer had slipped in and out of the bedroom window, it meant the killer would have had to find an escape route, a way to get from the second floor to the first without being seen. Not an easy thing to do.

"Gene," Addison said, "do you know what happened? Can you tell me?"

Absorbed in his own emotions, he didn't seem to hear her.

Police would be arriving soon.

If she was to get information beforehand, she needed to push harder.

Addison sat in front of him on the floor. "The police will be here soon, along with the medics, and who knows what they'll do. You were standing over Catherine when she died, which means you'll be taken in for questioning, at the very least."

Tears pooled in his eyes. "What happened wasn't my fault. I've never harmed a hair on her head."

"If you want us to believe you, we need to know what happened."

"I ... I don't know. I found her like this, on the floor, bleeding."

"The bedroom door was locked, though. And you were the only one in the room with her. If you didn't harm her, how is it possible that it could have been someone else?"

Face somber, he met Addison's gaze. "I didn't know the door was locked until you pounded on it."

"If you didn't lock it, then who did? Catherine?"

"I don't know."

"A man came to see Catherine today. Who is he?"

"What man?"

Addison shrugged. "I don't know, you tell me."

"I didn't know anyone else was at the house today. How long ago?"

Addison glanced at her cell phone. "About an hour."

"What did he look like?"

Addison described the man to Gene, relaying what little part of the conversation she'd overheard when she passed. "Does this sound like anyone you know?"

He shook his head. "Maybe. I don't know."

"Did anyone want to harm Catherine? Has she had problems with anyone lately?"

"I don't know."

I don't know seemed to be the only thing he knew how to say.

The wheels were turning, only they weren't going anywhere.

Tick, tock.

"I'm going to need a better explanation than you responding to everything with 'I don't know.' Help me understand what happened here, and why you think it happened."

He banged his head against the wall, expressing his frustration. "I told you, I don't know why she's dead. I wasn't here when it happened."

"If you weren't here, where were you?"

"There are stairs in this room. They lead to my private study on the first floor. I spend my afternoons there, take a little time to myself."

Stairs *inside* the bedroom?

Addison glanced around. She saw no stairs, and no other way out. What he was saying made no sense. "There are stairs *in here*? Where?"

It took a few tries before Gene mustered the strength to push himself into a standing position. "Follow me. I'll show you."

CHAPTER 22

Addison, Lia, and Marjorie followed Gene to a walk-in closet. He tugged on a string, and the room lit up.

"There," he pointed.

On the opposite wall was another door.

"I don't understand," Addison said. "Why have a secret door leading from this room to the study? Why not use the main stairs like everyone else?"

He moved a hand to his hip. "Catherine's grandfather, Luther, built this house."

"She didn't say much about Luther, but she talked about her father, Clayton."

"Clayton was a tyrant, the kind of man most people went out of their way to avoid. I don't think he started off that way though. His mother died when he was only ten. Then his father took over and proceeded to suck out all the sweetness his mother had instilled in him."

"So Luther installed the secret passageway?"

He nodded. "He may have been an abhorrent man, but he had a higher level of intelligence than most. He had a great love for books, non-fiction in particular. He built a small library in the study and turned it into a place of refuge, a place he could go in the morning without walking through the main house."

"Why go to the trouble and expense of creating a shortcut?"

"Luther had no interest being around people, and he had little tolerance even for those closest to him. Most saw him as ornery and distant, but after hearing various stories about him over the years, I'm convinced he was bipolar and socially awkward."

It was hard to believe. "I can't imagine what it must have been like for Catherine's father to grow up around him."

"Luther tolerated his children and his wife. It was everyone else he abhorred, his wife's parents in particular. She came from a tight-knit family who preferred spending time together than anything else. They loved the ocean, and they visited often, sometimes staying for weeks at a time, which infuriated Luther."

"Why not forbid them to visit, or ask them to stay for shorter periods of time?"

"The last few years of his wife's life, she was quite ill. Having her mother around brought her a great deal of comfort. He may have been an ill-tempered man, but he loved his wife, so he found a way to fulfill her needs by fulfilling his own. He installed a private staircase leading from this room to his personal study to ensure he interacted with her family on a minimal basis, and he made it clear to everyone that he was not to be disturbed when he was there."

Luther's story was fascinating, and while it explained how Gene entered the bedroom, it didn't exonerate him from murdering his wife. "I guess the thought on all of our minds is—*someone* murdered Catherine. If it wasn't you, then whom could it have been?"

He shook his head. "I wish I knew. Believe me."

"Take me through what happened before you found her."

"I was in the study watching a movie. I came upstairs to use the bathroom. When I walked through the closet, I heard someone talking to Catherine. Sounded like a man's voice, but I honestly don't know for sure. We don't have any men who work here on a regular basis aside from Brad, so at first I thought it was either Colin or that your husband had returned."

"Where is Brad now?"

"It's his day off."

"What about Colin? Where is he?"

"Not here. Catherine sent Whitney to the store, and Colin went with her."

"So you came through the closet door. Then what?"

"I heard her scream. It's a sound I'll never forget. The last time she screamed like that was when she collapsed the day our son died."

"What did you see when you came into the room, and what did you hear?"

"It sounded like, I mean, I swore I heard footsteps outside like someone was walking on the roof, but when I looked out the window, no one was there. It was then I realized the window was open, which seemed odd."

"Why?" Addison asked.

"Catherine was always cold. She never opened any windows in the house unless she was wearing a sweater, and today she was only in a short-sleeved shirt. There's no way she would have opened the window without putting her sweater on."

"What happened after you looked out the window?" Addison asked.

"I saw Catherine on the ground. I didn't even realize she was bleeding at first. I thought she'd fallen. Then I noticed her hand was pressed against her chest. When she saw me she reached out, and that was when the wound she'd been protecting opened. Blood spilled out of her. I was in shock. Everything became a blur. I knelt in front of her, and when I looked up, you and your grandmother were in the room."

A car door slammed shut outside, and then footsteps were heard in the hallway. Addison assumed it was the police until she heard Whitney's melodic voice. "Catherine, I have the body wash you asked me to get from the—"

Whitney and Colin entered the room holding a few paper sacks in their arms. Upon seeing Catherine covered in blood, Whitney buried her head in her hands.

Colin rushed to Catherine's side. "What's happened?"

"She's dead," Marjorie said.

"No. I can't believe it."

"There's more," Addison added. "We believe she was murdered."

"What?" Colin said. "How? Why would anyone want to kill her?"

"We don't know. An ambulance is on the way, and the police have been contacted."

"No disrespect," Colin said, "but where were all of you when it happened?"

"I beg your—" Marjorie said.

"It's a fair question, Gran," Addison interjected, "and one best answered by telling Colin and Whitney what we know up to this point. Although, it isn't much."

Addison talked through the events. By the time she'd finished, Whitney was sobbing, and Colin had pulled his wife into an embrace, doing his best to console her.

The sluggish, persistent whine of the ambulance drew near, the sand in the hourglass of Addison's ability to ask questions trickling to an end. But there was still time for one more.

"Gene, who would want Catherine dead?"

Gene took Catherine's hand in his, pressing it against his cheek. "She's cold. So cold now. And I was helpless to save her."

CHAPTER 23

A slender, dark-haired man in his mid to late forties entered Catherine's bedroom, his intense, haunting eyes tipping toward her in quiet observation. He stopped in a wide-legged stance, rubbed a hand across his chin, and stood in silence for a time, pondering. He then glanced at Addison, holding her gaze just long enough for her to realize who he reminded her of—a younger Al Pacino.

He shook his head, frowned, and said, "Oh, Catherine. What a shame," before removing his cellphone from his pocket.

Then he made a call. "Yeah, this is Lancaster. I'm going to need O'Shea over here right away."

He paused, listening to the chatter on the other end of the line, which seemed to irritate him. "I don't care where O'Shea is right now. Find him and get him over to the Ravencroft's place. And where the hell is Beck? He should already be here."

There was a brief reply, and then Lancaster ended the call.

A stocky, oval-faced female EMT with curly, ash-blond hair twisted into a thick, loose bun on top of her head rushed into the room.

Lancaster said, "Hey, Brie."

"Hey," she said.

She glanced over her shoulder into the hall and huffed in frustration. A minute later, a second police officer entered the room, a pint-sized bald man with a narrow, pointy nose and a sizeable beer gut. He paused in the doorway, leaning against the doorjamb with a hand pressed to his chest, panting like the stairs had been the only workout he'd had in quite some time.

He looked at Lancaster and said, "Sorry for the hold up."

"At least you're here now, Beck," Lancaster said.

Brie tapped Gene on the shoulder. "Excuse me, sir. I'm going to need you to move."

He didn't.

She snapped her fingers in front of his face. "Yo, sir. You hear me? I said I need you to move. Now. Mmm… kay?"

"He's in shock," Lancaster said. "Go easy on the guy."

He placed a hand on Gene's shoulder. "Gene, can you back up for me, please, and let Brie do her job?"

Gene released Catherine's hand and slid back.

Brie dropped to Catherine's side and checked for a pulse.

"You don't need to bother," Lia said. "She passed nine minutes ago. I assessed the wound and found—"

"I don't need any help, thank you," Brie hissed. "I know what I'm doing."

"I'm not offering *help*," Lia replied. "I'm offering facts."

Sensing the escalating tension, Lancaster cut in. "Ladies. Let's keep it friendly. There's no reason we can't all help each other."

Brie rolled her eyes and hissed again. "Fine. Can I do my job now?"

While Brie pretended to let it go, Lia could not.

"Just so we're all clear, I'm a medical examiner in Rhinebeck," Lia said. "Based on the size of the entry wound, I believe Mrs. Ravencroft was stabbed."

"Did you find anything to back up your theory?" Lancaster asked.

"We've had a look around," Lia said, "but we haven't found anything so far."

"We've been trying to piece together what happened," Addison said. "There hasn't been time to do much else."

"Not a problem. I'll take care of it." He bent down until he was eye level with Gene. "How are you holding up?"

Gene said nothing.

"You want to tell me what happened here, buddy?" Lancaster said. "I can't do much to help you until I know."

Gene took a deep breath in. "Doesn't matter what happened, Aaron. It just doesn't matter. Nothing does. She's dead."

"It's okay. Take some time. We'll talk again later." Lancaster stood and turned toward Beck. "All right, let's divide these two groups up, ask some preliminary questions."

Beck nodded.

Lancaster swiped a finger through the air, rounding up Addison, Lia, and Marjorie. "I'll take these three. You take the other two."

Whitney and Colin followed Beck out of the room.

"Ladies, let's talk in the hall," Lancaster said.

Addison, Marjorie, and Lia followed him out of the room.

"What about Gene?" Addison asked.

"Oh, he'll be all right."

"How can you be sure?"

"He's not going anywhere. We know each other."

That much was obvious.

"*How* do you know him?" Addison pressed.

"He played football with my father in high school. They've been friends for many years."

Lancaster exchanged glances with Addison and seemed to pick up on her concerns. Favorable treatment was being given to Gene, a man who may have been guilty of killing his wife.

He poked his head inside the bedroom. "Brie, keep an eye on Gene, will ya?"

"Anything *else* you expect me to do while I'm at it?"

"Improving your attitude would be a great place to start."

Lancaster reached into his pocket, pulling out a small notepad and a pen. "All right then, let's get everyone's names."

They each stated their name, and he took them all down.

"Fine," he continued. "Which one of you wants to tell me what happened?"

Addison raised a finger, quickly realizing the gesture made her feel like a child in elementary school. She lowered it. "I will."

He kicked his heel against the wall and leaned back. "All right, then. Go ahead."

Addison relayed the previous hour's events.

When she finished, he said, "So … no one knows who the possible mystery man was in Catherine's room earlier?"

Addison shook her head. "I didn't get a look at him, and according to Gene, Catherine never told him who stopped by today."

"And that's it? Anything else I should know?"

"What we know, you know," Marjorie said.

"I'll need to get your statements. Are all of you from Rhinebeck, or just Lia?"

It was a tricky question to answer. While Addison and Lia resided in Rhinebeck, Marjorie didn't reside anywhere. In recent years, she'd taken up the life of an expat, preferring to travel the world than to anchor to any one place for a length of time. Rather than explain, Addison did what Marjorie was already doing. She nodded.

"As soon as O'Shea gets here, we'll head down to the station," Lancaster said.

"Who is O'Shea?" Addison asked.

"The medical examiner."

"And you?"

"Detective. Like I was saying, we'll head to the station. I'll take your statements and question you individually. Until the medical examiner looks her over and I do a sweep of the house, you three will need to stick around the area."

His last comment seemed to be directed at Lia, and had been sweetened with a smile, which seemed to serve as a hopeful cherry on top. Over the last several minutes, Addison had noticed the more Lancaster spoke, the more his eyes wandered to Lia. And given the number of times Lia had swished the same lock of hair behind her ear, not only was she aware of his gawking, she welcomed it.

"We're happy to stay as long as you need," Lia said. "Whatever we can do to help."

"Speak for yourself," Marjorie said. "I don't want to be here any longer than I need to be. I'd like to get on with it and be on my way."

From the window in the hall, Addison watched a truck come to a stop next to Lancaster's squad car. Lancaster stood next to her, leaning toward the window to get a closer look. "Good. O'Shea is here. Moving on."

He checked in on Gene, who looked like someone had stuck a pin in him and let all the air out. "Ladies, if you wouldn't mind following me to the station, I'd appreciate it. In the meantime, I'll see what I can do about getting Gene into the car with me."

"And if he doesn't want to go?" Addison asked.

"It's obvious you have reservations about my relationship with Gene, so let me be clear. I have known him for a long time, and I can understand why you may believe I'd bend the rules because of it. I won't. I will treat him fairly, just like I would anyone else. That said—given the length of time I've known him compared to the few days you have, I can assure you he's no killer."

"I'd like to believe he isn't, either, but right now there's no other explanation as to what happened to Catherine, and while Gene's story is plausible, there's nothing to suggest anyone else is responsible."

"You're right. There's also nothing to suggest one or all of you *isn't responsible*, and yet for now, I've chosen to believe you're being honest with me. Give O'Shea some time. See what he comes up with. He's good. And so am I."

"This is a small town," Addison said.

"A town not unlike your own."

"Exactly. And in small towns, detectives don't see many cases of murder. Have you ever dealt with a homicide before?"

"Only one, but I think you'll find I know what I'm doing."

CHAPTER 24

Statements were taken, and then Lancaster segregated the women, calling Marjorie in first. Next was Addison's turn. He saved Lia for last, and when the door swung open after they'd finished, she bounced out of the room, flashing Lancaster a hearty grin.

"We need to discuss accommodations," Lancaster said.

"What are you talking about?" Marjorie said.

"I can't allow you to stay at the manor, not until I have finished gathering evidence. I'm sorry."

The inconvenience was too much for Marjorie to bear. "We haven't done anything. There's no reason to punish us by forcing us out of the Ravencroft's home. It's not *our* fault she's dead."

Lancaster raised a brow. "I'm not trying to *punish* anyone. It's an active crime scene. These things take time."

Marjorie moved a hand to her hip. "How much time?"

"Depends on what we find. I have two of my men over there now, and when I'm done here, I'll join them. The sooner I'm finished, the sooner you all can return to your homes."

O'Shea bolted into the police station. He looked to be around Addison's age—mid-thirties, she guessed. He had ginger hair, a trimmed beard, and was heavily freckled. In another lifetime, he could have been her brother.

His eyes darted around the room, coming to rest on Lancaster. "I need to talk to you."

"All right." Lancaster turned toward Addison. "This shouldn't take too long. You three sit tight."

The office door closed, and Addison elbowed Lia in the rib. "So ... Detective Lancaster's not bad looking, eh?"

Lia laughed. "Umm, I guess so. Why?"

"You know why."

"I don't know," Lia said. "I mean, there's a spark. We both feel it. But he's a bit old for me, I think."

"Too old?" Marjorie said. "Nonsense. It's all about intellect and maturity, and he has both. Ask me, older is wiser, and far better than wasting your time on some silly young'un you can't have a decent conversation with."

Although Lancaster's office had see-through glass walls on two sides, there was a tinted section in the middle prohibiting outsiders from looking in. Squatting down, Addison's view was limited, but she could see some of what was taking place. "Seems like he's found something."

"O'Shea?" Marjorie asked.

"Yeah, he just showed something to Lancaster."

Moments later, Lancaster opened the door and stuck his head out, calling for a man named Gordon, who popped out of a room nearby.

"Yeah?" Gordon asked.

"Find Beck. I've tried his cell, and he's not answering. I need Gene Ravencroft brought to me."

"Sure thing," Gordon said.

Lancaster tipped his head toward Addison. "I can see you, you know, peering into my office."

"I'm not sure what you're—"

"Yes, you do. Stop. Got it?"

Beck rounded the corner with Gene.

"Everything okay, Aaron?" Gene asked.

"No, Gene," Lancaster said. "'Fraid not. Can you come in here please?"

"Will I be able to go home today?" Gene asked.

"I don't know. Let's talk first."

Gene reached inside his pants pocket, fishing out the keys to the manor. He offered them to Addison. "In case I don't make it back tonight."

"They can't stay there, Gene," Lancaster said. "It has to be cleared first."

"All right." Gene pointed at the third key on the ring. "This one is for the guesthouse next to Colin and Whitney's place. You're welcome to stay there."

"Thank you."

She reached for the keys, and Gene's lips parted like he was about to speak. But then he hesitated.

"What is it?" she whispered.

He leaned in, the warmth of his breath tingling in her ear as he uttered, "Three eighty Mulberry Road."

CHAPTER 25

Addison did her best to focus on the road, but her mind was elsewhere, thinking about the address Gene had given her at the police station. What was there? Or who? Had Gene known something he hadn't told anyone yet? And if so, why tell her and not Lancaster?

If Gene wasn't responsible for Catherine's murder, maybe he knew who was. For now the mysterious address would have to remain just that, a mystery, until she could break free from Lancaster's watchful eye. At present he was in the car in front of her, gazing at her and Gran through the rearview mirror.

"Would you just look at her," Marjorie said, pointing to Lia who sat next to Lancaster in his squad car. "She doesn't seem to mind the difference in their ages *now*, does she?"

Addison gazed at the round, oversized sunglasses occupying half the real estate on Marjorie's face. "She seems to have embraced it. I'm happy for her. She deserves a good guy in her life."

"The little hussy can't stop staring at him, and she's grinning so wide you could run laps inside that mouth of hers."

"She's *not* a hussy, Gran."

"Oh, I know she's not. She's soft and gooey. Sensitive, kind of like you."

It almost sounded like a compliment.

"Well, good for her," Marjorie continued. "Maybe this is just what she needs."

Marjorie put her blinker on.

"And what do you think she needs, Gran?"

"A man who can loosen her up a bit, much like Luke did for you. The girl is wound tighter than a Tootsie Roll wrapper."

Addison supposed Lia was on the rigid side at times, but she made up for it with a plethora of other notable qualities. She was the most selfless person Addison had ever known—a good friend she could rely on.

"You were quiet when you got in the car," Marjorie said. "What's on your mind?"

Lots of things.

"I want to know what O'Shea said to Lancaster. Whatever it was, they seem to be keeping Gene overnight. Did you see the way Lancaster looked at Gene when he saw him in the hallway? It was like he knew what he needed to do, but he didn't want to do it."

"Maybe Gene's not the sweet man people in this town seem to think he is. Maybe he *did* kill his wife."

Addison was certain Cora was tied to the recent events somehow, that the present was a result of something that had happened in the past. "Let's say it wasn't Gene though, and the story he told about hearing someone else in the room is true. The question is—who else could it have been? Colin was with Whitney, and the gardener isn't working today. There must be someone else, which leads me to believe Gene knows something we don't. Maybe that's what he was trying to tell me."

"Why wouldn't he have told us before when he had the chance?"

"Who knows?" Addison said. "It's frustrating. I'm supposed to help spirits cross over, not play detective."

"Troubled spirits are never easy, I've found. Their situations are almost always complicated. That's why they're still here."

Lancaster made a turn. They were almost back to the manor. Luke would arrive soon. Telling him about the recent developments would put him on edge, but she didn't have a choice. Once she told him about Catherine, he'd push to take her home, expecting her to forsake Cora, which wasn't an option. Cora had made contact, and she wasn't going away until her needs were met.

"You're holding out on me, you know," Marjorie said.

"In what way?"

"You never told me what Gene said to you when he handed you the keys."

"He gave me an address. I have no idea why, or whether it's a place in town, or even in this state. Once we can shake Lancaster, I'll look it up. In the meantime, I need to talk to him."

"Gene?"

"Lancaster," Addison said.

"Why?"

"If his father is close to Gene, I'm guessing he knows the Blackthorn family history. Maybe if I get him talking, he'll tell me something I don't already know."

"Speaking of Lancaster, he seemed uneasy when Gene whispered that address to you. What did you say when he asked you about it?"

Addison shrugged. "What makes you think I didn't tell him the truth?"

"You're my granddaughter, and you're selective. You tend to withhold information unless it benefits you to reveal it. Otherwise, you're a vault of secrets."

Addison preferred the word "cautious" to "selective," but Marjorie was right. "I told him Gene mumbled, and it was too hard for me to understand what he said. It isn't a complete lie. Even now I'm not sure I heard him right."

"It's strange that he blurted out the address like he did."

"What bugs me is why he said it at all. Why not tell someone else—someone he knows and trusts?"

"You won't have an answer until you're able to check it out for yourself. I'll tell you one thing though—the guesthouse isn't big enough for all of us, not once Luke gets back."

"It's just temporary. We need to play nice, for now."

Marjorie rolled her eyes. "I'm too old to play nice. Who knows how long they'll take figuring out what happened. We need to speed things along, do some digging, and for that, we'll need access to the manor."

Marjorie was right.

Her wedding day had been full of unwelcome surprises.

She'd do whatever it took.

Nothing was getting in the way of her honeymoon.

CHAPTER 26

Addison and Marjorie followed Lancaster into the estate, parking behind him. Lancaster exited the car, and his phone jingled. He pressed it to his ear, his facial expression shifting from shock to elation. The topic of conversation seemed to be centered on Gene, but Addison couldn't make out any other details than that.

Marjorie and Lia headed inside, and Addison lagged behind, hoping this was her chance to speak with Lancaster alone. As if he sensed she was lingering, Lancaster met Addison's gaze. She decided to busy herself by opening the trunk of Marjorie's car and shifting items around in an effort to make it appear like there was a reason she remained outside. When she felt she had successfully pulled it off, she pushed the trunk closed, shocked to find Lancaster hovering over her.

"Find whatever it is you were looking for in there?" he asked.

"I … ahh … yeah."

He glanced at her empty hands, grinned, and said, "Really? Because it seems to me you're out here for a different reason. Care to share why?"

"I noticed you were on a call and heard you say Gene's name. I guess I just wondered if everything is all right."

"It is," he replied.

If she expected more, she'd need to do better. "What I mean to say is, is everything all right with Gene? I assume O'Shea found something."

He paused, eyeing her curiously. "You know, for a woman who is only here as a guest, you seem a little too interested in what's been going on."

"Until you know who's responsible for Catherine's death and why she was murdered, not only are we all suspects, I question whether we're safe. And for now, we can't even leave. If I knew what you knew, maybe I could help in some way."

It was a big ask, but he seemed to be considering it.

"Over the past few days, I had the chance to get to know Catherine," Addison added. "We had several conversations, and I'd like to think we were becoming friends."

"Catherine wasn't the friendly type, and not the kind of woman who usually made new friends. Aside from Gene, the only people I've ever seen her interact with on a personal level are the couple in the guesthouse. You mind explaining how you managed to get through to her in such a short time?"

"I just kept talking about things she cared about—her family, her life, the manor."

"Why?"

"Why not? The place intrigued me, made me want to know more. Beneath her hard exterior, I saw a woman wanting to connect. She just no longer knew how to do it."

"And did you … connect?"

"We talked about Billy, her son."

Lancaster rubbed a hand across his chin. "Billy. Wow. I haven't heard anyone say his name for a while now. I have two boys myself.

Can't imagine what it would be like to lose one of them. What happened to him was unfortunate. A terrible accident."

"Catherine said she blamed Cora for Billy's death."

"It was easy for her to place the blame on Cora, and I guess I see Catherine's logic. If Cora hadn't ended her life the way she did, he'd probably still be alive."

"I only know bits and pieces. I know Joseph died at sea, leaving Cora brokenhearted, and Cora couldn't live without him. Do you know what happened?"

"S'pose I can tell you what my father told me, and what I've heard over the years."

He glanced over his shoulder, noticed Lia and Marjorie peeking through the parlor window.

"Those two are supposed to be packing their things," he said, "not wandering around."

"We could go inside and talk there."

He nodded. "Good idea."

They walked to the manor, which gave Marjorie and Lia adequate time to take a hint and vanish. Beck was in the parlor, milling around.

"How's it going?" Lancaster asked.

"Fine, I guess."

He seemed confused, leading Addison to believe it may have been the first homicide scene he'd ever processed.

"Are you about done in here?" Lancaster asked.

"Think so."

"Good. I need the room."

Beck nodded and shuffled away.

Lancaster paced a moment. "Joseph and Cora married young. Right after they graduated. They were high-school sweethearts, but Cora, Catherine, Joseph, and Raymond had known each other since they were kids. They used to play together. When Joseph told Clayton he had proposed to Cora and they planned to marry, it came as no surprise, but his father didn't take the news well. He was against the marriage."

"Why was Clayton opposed to it? Did he have a problem with Cora?"

He shook his head. "He liked Cora. I imagine it was because she had a sweet temperament. From what I know about her, she never said a cross word about anyone. She tolerated Clayton, and most people didn't."

"Why would he be against the marriage, then?"

"Clayton had done a business deal with Cora's father the year before. I don't know the specifics, but it went south. Clayton blamed its failure on Cora's father, and Cora's father blamed it on him. It caused bad blood between the two families."

"Joseph and Cora still married, though."

"He would have married her no matter what his father said, but shortly after their engagement, Cora's parents died in a car accident, and Clayton softened, taking Cora under his wing like she was his own daughter. I also think he was trying to repair the damage he'd done. He'd already lost one son. He didn't want to lose another."

"When you say 'lost,' I assume you're referring to Raymond."

He nodded. "Raymond was hardheaded, just like Clayton. They bickered so much when Raymond was a teen, the kid dropped out of school and left town just to get away from him. He returned a few years later, right after Clayton passed away. He assumed, even though they weren't on good terms when he died, Clayton would leave the estate to him when he passed. He was wrong. Clayton managed to get one last dig in before he died. He cut Raymond out of his will completely, leaving the estate to Catherine and Cora."

"Cora? Why?"

"Toward the end of his life, when his liver was failing, it was Cora by his side day in and day out. He made an amendment to his will, stipulating Catherine and Cora were to take over the estate, and Joseph was to take over the fishing business."

"What did Raymond do when he returned and found out?"

"At the time, he was broke and had nowhere to go. Catherine took pity on him and invited him to move into the manor, which he did."

The pieces of Cora's life were finally starting to come together, but it was far more complex than Addison had imagined. So many questions remained. "Where is Raymond now? Is he still alive?"

Lancaster shrugged. "I don't know. Catherine and Gene haven't had any contact with him for many years. After Cora died, Raymond took off again. Took his daughter with him. Don't think he's ever returned."

"He left right after Joseph was lost at sea and Cora killed herself, I'm guessing?"

Lancaster eyed her curiously. "You know there's quite a time gap between those two events, right?"

She didn't.

"What do you mean?"

"Joseph disappeared five years before Cora committed suicide."

Five years?

It took a moment for it to sink in.

It couldn't be true.

Could it?

Addison thought back to the vision she'd had and how she watched Joseph's boat capsize and then Cora plummet off of the cliff with Billy in tow. Not once had Addison considered so much time had passed between the first event and the second.

"It doesn't make any sense," Addison said. "I was sure Cora's death followed Joseph's, that in her devastation, she walked off the edge of the cliff, killing herself, and Billy."

Lancaster shoved his hands inside his pockets. "Well, yeah, both of those events did happen, only at two different times. When Joseph's body was never found, Cora slipped into a depression. She barely spoke to anyone. This went on for months. Raymond thought Cora needed to move out of the manor, get away from it all. Catherine disagreed. She convinced Cora to stay and thought Cora would be better in time. She was wrong, and she paid the highest price for her mistake. S'pose there was no way they could have known, though."

It was human nature. One person believing the other could change and adapt because they themselves would change and adapt if put in the same situation. But no two situations are the same. No two people are the same either.

"The truth is, overcoming life's harshest challenges is hard," Addison said. "Cora's pain consumed her, and the day finally came when she couldn't bear it anymore."

"The ironic thing is, even though Catherine despised Cora over Billy's death, she still buried her in the family gravesite alongside the rest of the family, which means Catherine will join her now."

"Where is the family burial site—somewhere in town?"

"In town? No, it's a lot closer than you think." He tipped his head toward the back of the house. "It's back there, behind the guesthouses."

Behind the guesthouses on the estate was a fenced-in area Addison had wondered about. It was also padlocked, and the one time Addison had pressed her face to the wood, trying to peek between a thin, rectangular-sized crack between two slats, she'd felt the sharp thrust of a finger pushing into her backside. She'd turned to witness Catherine's disapproving look, which was followed by a lecture about the area being off-limits, not accessible to guests.

"Ah," Addison said. "It makes sense. When I arrived here, Catherine told me we could walk on the beach, but to stay away from the area past the guesthouses."

"I'm not surprised. For a long time, it was open. Then one night Catherine caught a few of the guests sitting on top of her parents' graves, smoking weed. The following week, she had the fence installed."

"I don't blame her."

"Yep, I don't either." He glanced into the hall. "Well, should we check on the others, see if they're all ready to go? You probably need some time to gather your things, too."

"I'm already packed. I had considered heading home today, well … before everything happened with Catherine. I'm just wondering, why share the Blackthorn's family history with me? I appreciate it, but I'm surprised. You don't know me."

"You're right. I don't. And you don't know me."

"Why do it, then?"

"I'd like to think I'm a good judge of character. I consider it part of my job. I believe you learn everything you need to know about a person by looking them in the eye."

What do my eyes say about me?

"You appear to be a good person with a genuine concern for others," he said. "You're kind, but troubled. Your mind is constantly wandering, just like it is right now."

"I've just had a lot going on this week."

"Your friend Lia thinks highly of you. She told me she's never met anyone with a heart as genuine as yours."

She'd watched the two of them step out of the car when they arrived back at the manor. As Lia headed into the house, she'd turned back, meeting Lancaster's gaze. Aside from Luke, she'd never seen a man look so smitten.

"You know, Gene told me something interesting today," he said.

"Oh?"

"On your wedding day, you were found unconscious on the porch."

"I was."

"You told everyone you'd fallen from the second-story window, even though no one saw it happen. Later, you said you'd been pushed out of it."

That's not possible.

Addison hadn't told Gene she'd been pushed from the window, so how did he know? And what else had he said to Lancaster? Maybe Addison's conversation with Lancaster was the opposite of what it appeared to be—less of an inquest about the Blackthorn family and more of a subtle attempt on Lancaster's behalf to get to know her when her guard was down.

Quid pro quo, Addison.

"I never told Gene I was pushed from the window," she said.

He grinned. "You're right. You *didn't* tell him. I hear the manor walls are thin. It seems like Gene has developed a habit of eavesdropping over the years."

Out the window, Addison watched Luke's car pull into the drive, the perfect time to cut the conversation short. "Well, thank you for taking the time to talk to me. I really appreciate—"

"Addison, if there's anything else I should know about what's going on here, I'm always available to talk. Even though we don't know each other, you *can* trust me."

Trust.

The ability to rely on someone other than herself.

It would take a lot more than words for him to earn that right.

"I'll keep it in mind," she said.

"And, oh, as to your question about Gene. The judge has agreed to release him on bail in the morning."

"Let me guess—the judge is a family friend too?"

"You don't need to worry. Gene's not a flight risk. He won't go anywhere."

Gene taking off wasn't what worried her. "You're keeping him overnight, though. You must suspect something."

"I did. And it's been disproven. A small amount of blood was found in Gene's car. It's not Catherine's, though; it's Gene's. Guess he cut himself a couple of days back."

How convenient. "Can I ask one last question?"

"Shoot."

"You mentioned Raymond left after Cora's death."

"Uh-huh."

"You also said he took his daughter," she said. "Was he married, because no one has even mentioned his wife?"

"Catherine didn't tell you?"

"Tell me what?"

Lancaster crossed his arms over his chest. "After his brother's death, Raymond spent most of his time taking care of Cora. Somewhere along the way they fell for each other, and about a year later, he married her, and they had a daughter together."

CHAPTER 27

The revelations kept coming, leaving Addison feeling like she was on the teacup ride, spinning in every direction. Cora had lived longer than Addison originally thought. And Raymond and Cora had married. Two unforeseen twists.

Had Cora *loved* Raymond? Or had the marriage been one of convenience, the consolation prize she'd accepted because he was familiar, and she knew he'd take care of her? And what of Raymond? Had he loved Cora? And why was this the first time she was hearing of it?

Marjorie descended the stairs, suitcase in hand.

"I still think this is a ridiculous waste of time," she said.

"Gran, can you do me a favor?" Addison asked.

"Depends on the favor."

"You know the fenced area toward the back of the estate?"

"Yes, yes, what about it?"

"Lancaster told me it's the family's graveyard, and I want to check it out."

"What does this have to do with me?"

Addison pointed out the window. "Can you distract Luke? Not for long, just for a few minutes while I take a look."

Marjorie set her suitcase down. "It's locked, you know."

Addison winked. "I know. I'll find a way."

While Marjorie went out the front door, Addison went out the back, tripping over Brad as soon as she stepped outside. He had been on his knees, pulling weeds. She hadn't seen him.

Catching her breath, she said, "Oh, hey, Brad. I didn't see you. I … ahh … didn't know you were back here. It's almost dark. I didn't think you worked today."

He dropped a handful of weeds into a black plastic bag. "I don't, usually. Needed something to keep my mind off what's happening. One of the officers called me wanting to ask a few questions. I told him I was here working, and since he was already on his way over, he met me here. I'm just finishing up. Where are *you* going in such a hurry?"

"We're being moved to the guesthouse tonight, I guess, until Lancaster says we're allowed to go home. I wanted to check it out, make sure it will work for all of us."

He frowned. "Sad what happened, isn't it? Catherine was always good to me."

It was clear Brad was in the mood to talk, but Addison wasn't. Time was limited. "It *is* sad. I actually think I would have liked her if I had the chance to get to know her more. I gotta go, but we'll catch up later, okay?"

Before he had the chance to add anything further, Addison took off. She reached the guesthouses, pausing a moment to ensure Brad didn't see her walk behind them, but he was no longer in sight.

Arriving at the wooden gate to the graveyard, she realized something.

The padlock securing the gate was gone.

Searching the soil beneath her feet, she noticed a smooth,

reflective piece of metal. She picked it up, palming it in her hand. The lock had been cut from the looks of it—sliced clean through. Addison bent down to find it, locating the missing fragment about six inches from the gate.

Addison had been in this exact spot one day earlier, and the lock was secure, which meant it had been broken in the last twenty-four hours. She pushed the gate open, expecting to find an ornate shrine of graves on the other side, but was met with simple headstones lined up in rows. And while they were nothing special, they were clear of weeds, and the headstones had all been wiped clean.

The first grave Addison came to was Luther's. He was buried next to his wife, Willimena, an infant boy who had died at birth, and a daughter who lived to the age of twenty-nine. Heading to the second row, her attention was diverted to a small headstone sitting off to the side, away from the others. A teddy bear rested in front, and clutched in the bear's hands was a weathered red ball.

Billy.

Addison walked to the headstone, crouched down, and lifted the bear off the ground, holding it in her hands.

"I'm sorry we never got to play ball," she said. "But you have a better playmate now, and she's wanted to play with you for a long time."

She returned the bear and went back to where she left off, the row of Catherine's parents, Clayton and Hilda. Joseph was buried beside them, and the headstones ended there.

Lancaster had said Cora was buried with the others.

So where was she?

A weight came over Addison, a coldness piercing her skin. The feeling was familiar, and one she'd had before. She wasn't alone. She looked up, even though she already knew who was there.

Cora stood in front of a tree a small distance away from the rest of the graves, and it was then Addison realized why Cora hadn't been placed with the rest of the family. Cora had been buried off to the side, a possible slight on Catherine's part, a way to shun her.

Unlike the other graves in the yard, Cora's was noticeably different, and it provided Addison with an answer to the question about why the lock on the gate was broken, and why someone was so determined to get in. Spanning the entire length of Cora's grave was something puzzling, something put there by someone else, someone living: dozens of bright, fresh-cut flowers.

CHAPTER 28

I was hoping you'd come," Addison said.

Cora acknowledged Addison's presence with a slight nod, then shifted her focus to her own grave, marveling at the festive new addition.

"They're beautiful. Someone went to a lot of trouble to place these here," Addison said. "Do you know who?"

Cora nodded.

"Do you know why?"

Another nod.

"Will you tell me who left them there?"

This time Cora shook her head.

Why?

Why won't she tell me?

I have to try another way.

"I've seen more than just you and Billy since I arrived here," Addison said. "The present isn't always all I see. Sometimes I see the past too."

Cora blinked at Addison, intrigued.

"I saw Joseph in his boat," Addison continued. "I know what happened to him."

Cora's mouth dropped open, the susurration of her words spreading into the air. She attempted to speak, clasping a hand around her neck when her voice box failed. Silenced in death for decades, speaking came with great difficulty now.

"Try again," Addison said.

Cora made a second attempt, this time managing to squeak out two words. "Tell ... me."

"Joseph was caught in the storm. He was trying to get the boat under control, but the sail had ripped. A wave crashed down with such force it split the boat apart, shooting him into the air. When he came down, he was forced underwater. At first I didn't see him, but after a few minutes, I noticed he'd found his way to the surface and wrapped his body around a piece of debris that had broken off from the boat. He stayed alive for several hours, fighting to hang on, but he was weak, and the water must have been freezing. In the distance, I heard Raymond, but he was still too far away for Joseph to hear him coming, and Joseph couldn't hang on anymore. I believe he knew he was dying. He spoke a few words at the end— words I'm sure he wished you could have heard him say. He said he was sorry. He said he was trying to make it back to you."

Hoping her words brought Cora comfort and a sense of resolve, Addison was shocked when they had the opposite effect.

Cora released a long, agonizing moan into the air, which erupted into a feverish scream. Fisting her hands, she stretched them out to her sides and gazed up, shrieking at the sky. The gentle breeze gathered, becoming a chill, insatiable wind, spinning and growing, devouring Addison into its core. The winds surged faster and faster, scooping Addison off the ground. She grappled for a tree branch, hooking one of her arms around it, fighting to hold on.

"I can't help you this way, Cora!" Addison shouted. "I know it's hard to accept. I know the pain it has caused you all this time, and I'm sorry. It's hard to let go of the past, but you have to if you ever want to leave this place. Don't you *want* to move on? Don't you *want* to be with Joseph again? I'm sure he's waiting for you right now, waiting for you to go to him so you can be together."

"No! You … don't … see. You … don't … see … anything."

"What don't I see? Tell me!"

The wind's strength was too much, Addison's grip becoming less secure. Splinters from the tree's branch pierced Addison's skin, scraping her arm as she struggled to hang on. "Cora, please! You'll never get what you want this way. Anger won't bring him back. What's done is done."

Marjorie appeared as if she'd been there all along, holding the black book in her hands. "Enough, Cora! Stop this!"

"Bring … him … to … me," Cora demanded.

Marjorie tossed the book into the air, its pages opening, flapping in the wind. Addison saw Marjorie's lips move, but she couldn't make out her words. Marjorie finished and her mouth closed. The book slammed shut, falling back into Marjorie's waiting hands.

The wind died down again, and the sky cleared. Addison tumbled to the ground.

She looked around. Cora was gone.

Marjorie rushed to her side. "What on earth is going on?"

Addison motioned toward Cora's grave, and the flowers, which were now sprinkled all over the yard. "The lock on the gate was broken when I got here, and Cora's grave was covered in flowers."

Marjorie scanned the area. "There must be over two hundred here."

"I'm guessing whoever killed Catherine left them, which means whatever happened in the past is tied to the present. This isn't just about helping Cora move on, anymore, Gran."

Marjorie nodded. "Yes, there's much more going on here than we know. We need to leave this place, Addison. We need to leave this place soon."

CHAPTER 29

Lancaster joined Addison and Marjorie in the backyard. "When I told you the graves were back here, it wasn't an invitation to break in."

"I didn't," Addison replied.

"Then why is the gate open?"

"The lock was broken when I got to it." Addison dug into her pocket, depositing the lock into Lancaster's hand. "Here, see for yourself."

He inspected it. "Well, isn't that convenient?"

"It wasn't me. Like I said, it was already broken when I found it."

"What are you two doing back here anyway?"

"Why does it matter?" Marjorie said. "We've done nothing wrong."

Lancaster raised a brow. "You haven't done anything wrong ... yet."

"We haven't done anything wrong *period.*"

Lancaster glanced around the yard. "Where did all the flowers come from?"

Addison pointed at Cora's grave. "Someone left them on Cora's grave."

"Then why are they scattered all over the place?"

Realizing she should have just answered with a simple "I don't know," her mouth moved faster than her mind's ability to process. "There was a gust of wind, and it blew them around a bit."

"A gust of wind? Today? When? There hasn't been anything but a slight breeze."

"The point isn't why the flowers are in disarray," Marjorie said. "The point is someone placed them on Cora's grave deliberately. The bigger question you should be asking is: who put them there?"

He frowned, and Addison worried what he'd say next.

"I was just coming back here to let you know I'd like to take Lia to dinner."

Given the circumstances, it was the last thing Addison expected him to say.

"All right," Addison said.

"I need you two to get your things moved over to the guesthouse so I can lock up the manor," he said. "We're still not finished. I'll be back tonight, and I expect you all to stay out of there while we're gone. And by the way, Addison, your husband is looking for you."

CHAPTER 30

Keeping in mind the manor's walls were thin, and Lia was headed downstairs to leave for dinner when Addison entered the house, Addison decided a text message was her best option to get through to her privately. She passed Lia on the stairs and smiled.

"Is everything all right?" Lia asked. "Where were you?"

"In the backyard," Addison said. "I'll fill you in later."

"I thought the gate was locked."

"It was. It isn't anymore. When you get back, we can talk. I need to get my bags out of the house. Keep your phone close, okay?"

Lia nodded.

Addison entered her room and whipped out her phone.

Addison: *Be careful with him.*

Lia: *Lancaster?*

Addison: *Yes.*

Lia: *Why?*

Addison: *So much has happened, at this point I don't trust anyone.*

Lia: *But he's a detective, and a good guy, Addison. I can tell. You can't really think he's involved in all of this.*

Addison: *I'm as suspicious of him right now as he is of all of us. It goes both ways, believe me.*

Lia: *Okay, but I think you're overreacting.*

Addison: *And I think you're putting a lot of trust into a man you hardly know.*

Lia: *Really?!*

Addison: *I'm just worried about you being alone with him, that's all. He may be a detective, but he's human, just like everyone else.*

Lia: *He's given me no reason to suspect him of being anyone other than the person he is.*

Addison: *I'd like to know where you're going.*

Lia: *For dinner? I don't know yet.*

Addison: *Text me when you do, okay?"*

Lia: *Oh ... kay. I just think you're being ridiculous. And paranoid. It's just dinner.*

She was right.

It was *just* dinner.

Until it wasn't.

CHAPTER 31

"Where have you been?" Luke asked.

"I was behind the guesthouses," Addison said. "There's a family graveyard back there."

"I don't like what's going on here. I spoke to Lancaster, and I don't care what you feel you need to do for Cora, we're not staying."

"We can't leave, Luke."

"Actually, we can. It's not safe, and you know it."

Addison walked to the desk, grabbed a scratchpad and a pen, and wrote: *The walls in this place are thin. Anyone lurking around hears everything we say. Let's talk when we get to the guesthouse.*

Luke walked to the bedroom door, opened it, and looked into the hall. "No one's there. You're fine. Talk to me."

"No one's there *now*," Addison whispered. "Wait a few minutes, okay? Just long enough for us to get out of this house and for Lia and Lancaster to leave for dinner. Once it's just you, me, and Gran, we'll talk."

"What's going on with Lia and Lancaster anyway?"

Addison widened her eyes, and he waved both hands in front of him. "All right, all right. I get it. Message received. I'll wait."

CHAPTER 32

This place is too small," Marjorie said. "I'm not staying here."

"It's one night, Gran," Addison said.

"Well, I'm not sharing a room with Lia. She can take the couch."

Luke, who had been leaning against the wall with one leg crossed over the other said, "There's no point talking about it. We're going home."

"We can't," Addison said.

"If Lancaster has more questions, he can call. We're only a few hours away, Addison. He'll be fine."

"But he said not to leave."

"In this situation, I agree with Luke, Addison," Marjorie said.

Addison threw her hands in the air. "Thank you *both* for your support."

"It's not about support," Luke said. "It's about safety."

"I said I agree," Marjorie said, "and I do. However, Addison must see this through now. Cora will remain connected to her until it's over, until Addison does what she needs her to do so she can move on."

"It's one thing to help her," Luke said. "It's another to put herself in danger while doing it. First she's pushed out the window, and now Catherine is dead. We're no longer dealing with a spirit—we're dealing with a murderer."

"All I need to do is help Cora," Addison said. "Once I can get her to move on, I can leave, and the police can take care of the rest."

"I don't want you here any longer," Luke said.

Addison took Luke's hand in hers. "I know how much you want to protect me and keep me safe. I appreciate it, and I don't blame you. But we talked about this when we first started dating, and you made me a promise. Do you remember?"

He sighed, then nodded. "I swore I wouldn't interfere. It's different this time."

"Different doesn't invalidate your promise, though."

"The more these spirits contact you, the more you're at risk. The situations you're getting yourself into are starting to get out of hand. These spirits are still here because something tragic happened in their lives. Their tragedies create risk. You can't expect me to be okay with it. You deserve to be happy. You deserve a normal, happy life."

"I didn't choose this life. It chose me. I'll admit, it scares me sometimes, but I have to believe a higher power chose the women in my family for a reason and that I'll be protected when I need to be."

He shook his head and walked away. "I'm not sitting here listening to this anymore. I can't."

Addison started after him, and Marjorie grabbed her wrist, stopping her.

"Let me go to him, Gran," Addison said. "He's frustrated because of who we are."

"Stay here and get settled into the guesthouse," Marjorie said. "I'll go. It's time the two of us have a talk."

CHAPTER 33

Marjorie found Luke close to the lookout point where Cora had taken her life. He was talking to himself, ranting to the air like a lawyer engaged in a one-sided debate.

"It's not my wife's fault you refuse to move on, Cora," he said. "If you loved your husband the way I love my wife, then you'll understand my need to protect her. Keeping her here puts her life in danger. Do you care about the risky situation you've put her in, or do you only care about yourself? Addison has tried to help you, and you've refused it. Accept her help and move on, or leave her alone."

Startled, he looked back, surprised to see Marjorie nearby.

"Luke, can I talk to you?" Marjorie asked.

"How long have you been standing there, listening?"

"Long enough."

"Hell, I don't even know if these spirits can hear anyone except you and Addison, but it's worth a try. I thought if I stood at the place where she died, I might have a chance to reason with her. Can you see her? Is she here? Or am I just wasting my time?"

"I'm not sure."

"Why not? If she was here, you would see her, right?"

Marjorie dug a hand into her lower back, kneading away a sharp, persistent pain that had grown in intensity in recent days. "I'd like to continue this conversation, Luke, but as much as I despise admitting it, I'm getting too old to be on my feet all the time. I need to sit down."

"All right." He scanned the area. Seeing no acceptable options, he removed his jacket, setting it on the ground in front of a boulder. "There. How about that? It won't be comfortable, but it will give your back a rest."

She nodded, and they sat down.

"I need to tell you something," she said, "and it's important you know that I'm telling you *before* I've told Addison. I haven't found the right time to talk to her yet. Not that there is a right time or a wrong time for such things, but I would appreciate you keeping it to yourself, for now."

He scratched his head. "Depends on what it is, Marjorie. I don't like the idea of keeping secrets from her. You understand, right?"

She smacked him on the leg. "Of course, I do. It's one of the reasons I like you so much. You're good for her, and she needs you, more now than you realize."

"If you came here hoping to change my mind, it won't work."

Although his words were firm and honest, once she said what she'd come to say, she was sure it would change everything. "I'm not trying to change your mind."

"Why are you here, then?"

"I'm dying, Luke. Addison is my legacy … my family's legacy. Everything we are and continue to be relies on her."

"What do you mean—you're dying?" he said. "Are you sick?"

"I could be, I suppose. I don't like doctors. Haven't been to one in years."

"If you haven't seen a doctor, how do you know?"

"The abilities I once had are ebbing away. I feel them draining from me, and not just because Addison's have grown stronger. I can't see them anymore ... the spirits Addison sees. The ones I *used* to see. I should have been able to see Cora and Billy, and I can't. Addison suspects I've been keeping something from her. I haven't confirmed it."

"I guess I still don't understand. What does not seeing spirits have to do with dying?"

A soft breeze prickled Marjorie's fragile skin, producing tiny pimples of gooseflesh on her arms. She tugged on her scarf, tightening it around her neck. "When the gift we have to communicate with the dead passes from mother to daughter, or grandmother to granddaughter in this case, as Addison's abilities strengthen, mine diminish, but they don't vanish completely. Not until the end."

"Then what happens?"

"It might be best explained if I tell you a story from my past."

He shrugged. "All right."

"I was in my living room one afternoon. This was decades ago, before Addison was even born. Peter, Paul and Mary's "Blowin' in the Wind" was playing on the record player. I had a feather duster in my hand, and I was dancing around the house, dusting as I went along. Out the window, I saw my mother's white Jaguar pull into the drive. She parked and got out of the car, carrying a wallet in one hand and a thick black book in the other. I stared at the book as she walked, having no idea how much it was about to change my life."

"What book?"

"One I gave Addison earlier. It has been in our family for many generations."

"How did it change things for you?"

"After I invited my mother inside that morning, she handed the book to me and said it was time for me to have it. Unlike Addison,

I was familiar with it. On a couple of occasions, I had witnessed my mother using it. I knew if she had decided to give it to me, something was wrong. So I asked her."

"What did she say?"

"The opposite of what I expected. Instead of answering my question, she said she was sorry for not telling me she loved me more often over the years. She said she was proud of me, proud of the woman I'd become, and of the way I had parented Nancy, Addison's mother. My mother was a blunt woman, much like myself, so after she dispensed with the pleasantries, she looked me in the eye and said she wouldn't be around much longer. She said she was going to die."

"Did she say why?"

"A few weeks earlier, I had encountered a spirit at a hotel we stayed at, but my mother had not seen it, and usually she did. She said she knew her time was almost up because it had been foretold in the book."

Luke shook his head. "How?"

"The book is divided into two parts. The first half contains verses that, when read aloud, call on the spirits of our female ancestors. The second part is a guidebook, containing warnings and detailing things relevant to us. I planned on telling Addison, but she's been troubled over Cora, so I chose to show her the power within the book instead."

"How much time do you have, Marjorie?"

"I don't know. Eight days after I received the book, my mother died, so I assume I don't have long."

"What happened to her?"

Marjorie closed her eyes, replaying the events in her mind as if they had happened only yesterday. Even now she could smell the flowery aroma of her mother's perfume wafting through the air just like she had when she'd discovered her mother's lifeless body.

"Marjorie," Luke asked. "Are you okay? We don't have to talk about it, you know."

"No, no, it's all right. It's good for you to know these things. One morning my father went outside to get the newspaper. He passed my mother in the garden. She was watering her flowers just like she did each day. He gave her a little squeeze. The paperboy had done a poor job of tossing the paper into the driveway, and it had landed in the street. My father bent down to grab it. At the same time, one of their neighbors was driving in his direction. Her son was sitting in the back seat. He had taken the sucker he was eating out of his mouth and stuck it to the back of her hair. She turned to scold him and wasn't watching the road."

"Did she hit your father?"

"She would have, except my mother pushed him out of the way. The car hit her instead, and she died instantly."

"It would have happened in a matter of seconds though. How did she get to the street so fast unless she knew what was going to happen beforehand."

Marjorie offered a slight nod. "You're right. She did know. The night she passed, she visited me. It's the only time I've ever seen her since her death. When my father touched her in the garden that morning, she had a vision. She saw my father bending down in the street. She saw the distracted neighbor in her car. And she saw two possible outcomes. She had a choice to make—spare his life or spare hers. I believe when my time comes, something similar may occur. I'm ready, and I've made my peace."

"Addison has never had contact with her mother. Why were you visited, and she hasn't been?"

"Nancy refused her gift as you know—refused to engage with the spirits around her. It made her, well, mortal, like you. I suppose she isn't able to visit Addison."

Luke stood, faced Marjorie. "I knew about Nancy's rejection.

But I guess it never occurred to me that after Addison started seeing spirits, she could stop seeing them if she wanted to. Are you saying she doesn't have to live this life?"

"Addison had a choice, Luke, and she made it, which is why I'm here talking to you now. I need you to watch over her for me. I know how hard it is for you to accept, but it's her birthright, just like it will be your daughter's one day."

"If she gives it up, she can have a normal life. Why wouldn't I want that for her? Why can't all of this stop—right here, right now?"

"Then who will help all the lost souls trapped here with nowhere to go?"

"I don't know, but Addison shouldn't have to take it on herself. Why is it her job to help them?"

"It's much more than a job, Luke. It is her destiny, and neither you nor I have the right to deny her of it."

CHAPTER 34

Addison had been left alone, providing her a small window of opportunity. And she had something in mind—scouting the possible locations of the address Gene had given her. A quick search on her computer pulled up a few possibilities for 380 Mulberry Road, the closest being one in Bay Shore, which was less than an hour away. Luke wouldn't appreciate returning and not finding her there, but there were too many what-ifs to consider:

What if he was still angry after talking to Marjorie?

What if he asked her not to go?

What if he tried to stop *her* from going?

Lancaster and Lia would return at any time.

If she was going to slip out, she had to do it now.

She walked to Colin and Whitney's house and knocked on the door.

"Door's open," Whitney shouted. "Come on in."

Whitney and Colin were snuggled up together on the couch, watching a movie.

"Hey, guys," Addison said. "Sorry to bother you."

Colin craned his head toward Addison and smiled. "It's fine. Everything okay?"

"Yeah, I was just wondering if you had a piece of paper and a pen?"

Colin grabbed the television remote, paused the movie, and sat up. "Sure. Should be in the top drawer in the kitchen. Let's see here …"

He walked to the kitchen, opened the drawer, and gave Addison what she needed.

"Thanks."

"We thought a funny movie would help get our mind off … you know," Colin said, "everything going on around here. After it's over, we're making a cocktail, if you're interested. We have enough for everyone."

"I have to run out for a bit."

He glanced at the time. "This late?"

"Just a quick errand. But Marjorie and Luke would probably want to join you when they get back."

Addison returned to the other guesthouse. Now came the hard part, trying to decide what to say. She considered telling Luke and Marjorie the same thing she'd just told Colin and Whitney, but changed her mind, realizing it didn't feel right keeping the truth from them.

She jotted down a quick explanation:

Luke and Gran,

I couldn't stop thinking about the address Gene gave me earlier. (Luke, Gran will fill you in on the details). I did a search and noticed there's a Mulberry Road in Bay Shore. It's probably nothing, but since it's not a long drive, it's worth checking it out, and I didn't want to wait until tomorrow to do it. I apologize for not waiting and taking one of you with me. I have my cell, and I'll check in once I'm there and when I'm headed back.

xo Addison

CHAPTER 35

The house at 380 Mulberry Road was dark when Addison arrived. There were no lights on inside—nothing to indicate whether anyone was home. A single, dim streetlamp flickered off and on in three-second intervals, like the light bulb had a short in it. Addison checked the time on her cell phone. It was a few minutes past eight—still a bit early for people to head to bed.

On the drive over, she'd missed three calls—two from Luke and one from Marjorie. She texted them both saying she had arrived at the address Gene gave her, and she'd check in again in a few minutes. She'd left the note on the pillow in Marjorie's room. By now, Marjorie would have shared the information with Luke. She assumed they'd come after her, which meant she didn't have long.

She pressed on the doorbell. It chirped like a nightingale. Footsteps followed, someone drawing near. The porch light flickered on overhead, and the door opened just wide enough for the elderly man on the opposite side to stick his head out so he could get a good look at his visitor.

The man was dressed in a thick, maroon bathrobe and tennis

shoes with no socks, which seemed like an odd combination both in dress and for the time of night. He was taller than most men, towering at least a foot over Addison, and his oval-shaped head was smooth, without a wisp of hair on it. He looked very average with the exception of one thing—his eyes.

"You're Raymond, aren't you?" Addison asked. "Raymond Blackthorn."

He pulled a pair of glasses from the robe's pocket, pressed them onto the ridge of his nose, and opened the door a bit wider. "It seems you know who *I* am, but I can't say the same for you."

"My name is Addison Lockhart. I mean … Addison Flynn."

He eyed her curiously. "Which is it then, Lockhart or Flynn?"

"Flynn. Sorry. I just got married. We've been staying at Blackthorn Manor."

He sneered. "Well, now, that's a shame."

"Why?"

"I pity anyone who has to put up with my sister."

"Do the two of you have a bad relationship?"

"Sweetie, we don't have a relationship at all. Now, why don't we skip the pleasantries and cut to the part where you tell me what you're doing here? Did Catherine send you?"

Raymond talked about his sister in the present tense, as if he had not yet heard what had happened to her. "Gene sent me."

"Huh. I wasn't aware Catherine told him. She said she wouldn't. Never could trust her to keep anything from him, though."

"Told him what?" Addison asked.

"About me staying here."

"Isn't this your house?"

"In a manner of speaking. It once belonged to my brother, Joseph. He bought it as a surprise for Cora on their wedding day. Paid cash for it."

"Why would he buy this house when the manor was partially left to Cora in your father's will?"

He raised a brow. "Look at you, Little Miss Information. Catherine been squawking in your ear?"

She shook her head. "Actually, no. Lancaster told me."

"Lyle Lancaster?"

"Detective Aaron Lancaster. You didn't answer my question."

"Joseph didn't want to live on the estate. He wanted to start a life with Cora somewhere else, so he bought this place. They lived here and usually visited the manor on the weekends. Now you're all caught up."

Not even close.

"Did you and Cora live here when you were married?" Addison asked.

"What are you getting at, showing up here on my doorstep, dragging up the past, like you have a right to make my family business your own?"

Since Raymond behaved like he was in the dark about Catherine, Addison decided to keep the details of Catherine's murder to herself. For the moment, at least. "Your sister has been talking to me about buying the estate, and I'm interested in its history."

He didn't speak for several seconds. It made Addison nervous, wondering if the lie she'd just told was an obvious one.

"I don't know why you care so much," he said. "What's in it for me?"

The first lie worked.

Why not test another?

"Catherine's been talking about including you in the sale of the house, providing you with a monetary settlement once the deal goes through."

"And why would she do that?"

"She knows it was rightfully yours when your father died."

"Catherine never cared before, and she certainly didn't care this morning. Why the sudden change of heart?"

"She's had all day to think about it."

He laughed. "Huh. She told me she had a buyer, and the deal had been made. Never thought it was some youngster like you, though."

"Have you lived here all these years?"

He shook his head. "I tried living here after Cora's death. Thought this place would do me good. I couldn't handle it. Too many memories of Joseph and Cora, I guess. So I left, and this place has sat here like a time capsule ever since."

"When did you return?"

"A few months ago."

"Why?" Addison asked.

"My daughter Brittany became engaged recently, and she asked about taking over the house. I came back to get it all cleaned out for her so she can move in."

"Brittany. Catherine never mentioned her."

"Why would she? They don't have a relationship. Catherine wouldn't even recognize her if she saw her. The last time they were in the same room together, Brittany was only around four years old."

"I saw you at the manor today, arguing with Catherine in her room."

Unsure of his reaction, she'd taken a step back.

Raymond tightened the tie on his robe. The sleeve slid up, revealing a thick layer of gauze wrapped around his left arm. He noticed Addison sizing it up and shoved the sleeve back down. "I have to say, after all this time, I can't believe Catherine's selling the estate. Whether she wants to cut me in on the deal isn't the point. It should remain in the family. If you're in a hurry to purchase, you'll want to rethink your decision. I won't let it go without a fight."

"Are you saying you'd do anything to stop the sale?"

His stare was cold and calculating, eyes like a wolf sizing up his prey. "I'll do whatever it takes."

"Is that why you killed her?"

He stepped back, tipped his head to the side. "*Killed her?* What do you mean?"

145

"Don't act like you don't know about what happened to Catherine today. She's dead, Raymond, and you're the one who killed her."

CHAPTER 36

Raymond hit the floor like his body was a giant brick, his head smacking against the wall as he went down. Addison stood, hovering over him, thinking. At his age, he was far too old to scale Catherine's rooftop after her murder. Addison considered a secondary option. What if the open window had served another purpose? What if Raymond had opened it as a distraction? There was one hiding place Addison hadn't considered until now—the closet. It was possible Raymond had hidden behind a row of Catherine's clothes, waited for Gene to enter through the secret passageway and then used it as his escape route. And then there was the question of his bandaged arm. What if it hadn't been injured some other way, but because Catherine had defended herself against the knife?

She rushed to the car, skidding to a stop when she saw Cora's luminous apparition floating in front of the driver's-side door, shaking her head.

"You don't want me to leave?" Addison asked. "Why? What do you need me to do here?"

Addison thought back to the words Cora spoke in the garden: *Bring him to me.*

Had she meant Raymond, and not Joseph?

Cora floated past Addison, flicking her wrist, beckoning her to follow.

"He's dangerous, Cora. It's not safe for me to be here."

Cora drifted over Raymond, her head tilting toward a dresser in the foyer. Addison stood, fighting the urge to get in the car and speed away. Cora was agitated, desperate.

There was something Cora needed her to do here, which meant she couldn't leave. Not yet.

"All right, Cora. Hang on."

If she was going to stay, she needed to make a call first.

"Where are you?" Lancaster barked.

"In Bay Shore at 380 Mulberry Road. I found him."

"Slow down. Whom did you find?"

"Raymond. I think he killed Catherine."

"What makes you think … did he tell you he killed her? And what in the hell are you doing there by yourself?"

"He hasn't said he murdered her, not yet."

"What do you mean, *not yet?* Where is he now?"

"Passed out, I think, in the entryway. I asked him about Catherine's death, and he fainted."

Lancaster breathed a heavy sigh. "Addison, listen to me. If he *is* responsible, you need to get out of there. You need to get out of there right now."

CHAPTER 37

Addison stepped over Raymond and opened the dresser drawer. Inside she found a variety of tools, tape, a box of nails, and something useful—rope.

She scooped Raymond off the ground, struggling to lift him onto a chair. Still groggy, his eyes fluttered open and closed. He was coming around. She had to work fast. She wound the rope around him several times, knotting it behind him.

Cora floated to the side, watching.

Addison thought back to the moment at the police station when Gene had offered the address she was at now. His voice had been muffled and strained, and it hadn't sounded like him.

"Gene didn't give me the address to this place, did he?" Addison said. "You did. You spoke through him."

Cora nodded.

Addison secured the knot. "All right, Cora. Now what?"

Cora drifted down the hall, slipping into a bedroom. Addison followed. Everything was caked in a layer of dust like it hadn't been touched in decades, making Raymond's story of the house being vacant plausible. The bed was covered in a multi-colored patchwork quilt, which was edged in lace, and from the small, circular-shape indentation on the pillow, it appeared that this was indeed where Raymond had been staying.

The décor was simple. A pair of framed scenic ocean prints adorned the wall, and a group of candles were on the dresser next to a trio of small artificial plants in clay pots. Cora pointed at the plant in the center.

Addison picked it up. "I'm not sure what you want me to do with this."

Cora stared at the pot in Addison's hand until the inside began to glow. Addison pulled the plant out, hacking when dust spread through the air like pollen in the wind. She looked inside and saw an object at the bottom, an item preserved for many decades. A necklace.

Joseph's necklace.

CHAPTER 38

Addison slapped Raymond's face, jolting him awake. He glanced down, noticing the rope. "What's going on here? What are you doing? Why am I tied up like this?"

Addison bent the pot to the side, allowing him to see inside. "Recognize this?"

Raymond stared into the pot. "How did you know that was in there?"

"You told Cora you didn't find Joseph when you went out looking for him. You said all you found were pieces of the boat."

"What about it?"

"You lied."

"No, I didn't."

"Yes, you did. Joseph was wearing this necklace when he died. If you never found him, how do you have it?"

Raymond considered the question. "Who are you, really? A cop? A private investigator? You're wasting your time digging up the past."

"Answer the question."

"Whatever witch hunt you're on, I'm not the answer. Joseph wasn't the only one who had one of those necklaces. We both had one. Our father gave them to us. So how about you untie me and get the hell out of my house!"

Addison looked at Cora.

Cora shook her head.

Raymond was lying.

But she needed to be sure, needed to see for herself the rest of what happened the day Joseph disappeared.

CHAPTER 39

Addison closed her eyes and tipped the pot on its side, allowing the necklace to slide into her hand. When her eyes reopened, she was back at the wreckage site. Raymond's voice howled through the air, calling out to Joseph. Upon discovering Joseph's boat, he killed the motor, his boat sputtering to a stop. Raymond took out a pair of binoculars and scoured the water for his brother. Minutes passed, and then finally, he saw what he was looking for—Joseph, tired and worn, clinging to a piece of debris.

Raymond pulled alongside him and reached out, fishing him out the water. Once his brother was in the boat, he raced toward a bin and flipped it open, yanking out a blanket. He threw it around Joseph and pulled it tight. "Here, brother. It's okay. Get warm."

Raymond sat down next to him, waiting.

Several minutes passed in silence, and then Joseph said, "I didn't think you'd come."

"Yeah, well, maybe I didn't think you'd still be alive."

"A few more minutes, and I wouldn't have been. Disappointed?"

"You shouldn't have taken off like you did. It was stupid. You knew a storm was coming."

"I needed to clear my head," Joseph said.

"You mean you needed to go somewhere I wasn't … when you didn't get your way after we talked, right?"

"Something like that."

"Yeah, well, I can't give you what you want."

"You can," Joseph said. "You just won't."

Raymond sighed, reached inside a cooler, flicked the tab off a bottle of beer, and offered it to Joseph. "Want one?"

Joseph shook his head. "You kidding?"

Raymond shrugged and tipped the can toward his mouth, guzzling back a few swigs. "You're being unreasonable and paranoid. Cora picked you, not me."

"And yet you never miss an opportunity to put your hands on her."

"I'm her brother-in-law, and we've all been friends for a long time. Nothing has happened between us, Joseph. She loves *you*."

"And *you* love *her*. I meant what I said this morning. I don't want you coming around anymore."

"It's not your decision to make. It's Cora's. What do you think she's going to say when you tell her we can't see each other? You may be her husband, but I'm still her friend."

Joseph leaned back, closed his eyes. "She'll understand."

"If you believe that, you don't know your wife."

"I know she'd do anything to make me happy."

Raymond shook his head. "It's never enough with you, is it? You and your need to have everything go your way. I was with Cora first until you swooped in, or have you forgotten?"

"You were thirteen. It's not the same thing."

"Oh, so you being two years older made a big difference?" Raymond chugged the rest of the beer and reached for a second. "My feelings were every bit as real as yours, and I still stepped aside when her affection changed from me to you. I thought it would be enough for you, but it wasn't. You're hell-bent on cutting me out permanently."

"You disrespected me, Ray."

"How?"

"I see the way you look at her, the way you watch her walk across a room," Joseph said. "Everyone does."

"You're paranoid, little brother."

"I'm *right*," Joseph said.

"I won't walk out of her life."

"I've had time to run through it while I've been out here, thinking what would happen if I died today. You're toxic, Ray, just like Dad was. She acts like a different person when she's around you. You don't want to budge? Fine. I'll budge for you."

"What do you mean?"

"I'm putting our place up for sale when we get back," Joseph said, "We're moving."

"Where?"

"I haven't decided. Somewhere far from you."

"You wouldn't take her away from all of us."

"You mean I wouldn't take her away from *you*."

"Don't go ape, Joseph. We're her family. We're all she has."

"I'm wiped out, and I want to get back. Let's go."

"Not until we work this out."

Joseph stood. "Let's … go."

"What in the hell is wrong with you?"

Joseph headed to the front of the boat. "We're leaving."

Raymond jerked on the blanket, reeling Joseph back. The blanket caught on Joseph's necklace, tearing it off.

Joseph glared at it, then slugged a weak fist toward Raymond's jaw, narrowly missing him.

"You know something, Joseph? You're right," Raymond said. "You're an arrogant prick. I *shouldn't* have come looking for you."

Raymond slammed the beer bottle into Joseph's head, splitting it open. As blood spilled out, Raymond realized the irreparable damage he'd done, and he did the only thing he could think to do—he grabbed his brother and heaved him back into the water.

CHAPTER 40

"H" ey," Raymond said. "What's the matter with you? You on drugs or something?"

Addison's eyes opened, and for a moment, she stood in a haze, stunned. In her previous vision, Joseph had slipped beneath the water, leaving her to assume he was dead. But she had been wrong.

So wrong.

Raymond wriggled around in the chair, searching for a means to escape, but the rope was secured at the end with a tight, unrelenting knot, one her father had taught her when she was a teen. Raymond wasn't going anywhere.

Addison exchanged glances with Cora. "I saw him. I saw everything. I know what you need me to do now."

Cora nodded.

Raymond shouted expletives and cranked his head to the side, staring where Addison had just been talking. "What *is* this? There's no one there. Who are you talking to?"

Addison glared at him. "Do you really want to know? Because you wouldn't believe me if I told you."

"Uhh, try me," he snorted.

"Was it an accident, or were you trying to kill your brother, just like you killed Catherine?"

"Enough!"

"Joseph planned on moving to get Cora away from you, so you killed him. I can prove it. I'll tell you something no one else knows."

"You don't *know* anything."

"You rescued your brother the day of the storm, but then the two of you fought over Cora. He tried to punch you, and you sliced his head open with a beer bottle before pushing him into the ocean."

Raymond sat there, blinking at Addison, shocked.

"It's not … it's not possible," he said. "There's no way you could know about our argument. No one else was there."

"I'm right, though. It's true, isn't it? How long did you get away with it before Cora found the necklace?"

"What's your plan? You tie me up, call the police, and tell them about a cold case no one cares about anymore? Go ahead … call 'em. Say whatever you want. I'll be sure to let them know about you breaking into my house and holding me against my will."

She dangled the necklace in front of him. "It won't matter once I show them this."

"What, a piece of jewelry you allege my brother was wearing the day he disappeared?" he said. "No one can back up your story. Joseph's dead, and yeah, I killed him. And you wanna know the best part? No one will ever believe a word you say."

Lancaster stepped into the room, dipping his head toward Raymond. "Oh, I don't know about that, Raymond. I might."

CHAPTER 41

Raymond was cuffed and placed in the back of a Bay Shore squad car. Lancaster discussed the case with local police, and they made some calls, ordering a complete search of the house. Raymond had confessed to Joseph's murder, but not Catherine's. To convict him, they still needed to prove he was the one who did it.

"You mind telling me how you knew he murdered his brother?" Lancaster asked.

"I ... umm ... Catherine told me."

"*Catherine?*"

His expression indicated he didn't believe her, but it didn't matter. Catherine was dead. There was no way he could disprove her comment. "I think Catherine suspected Raymond killed Joseph for years, but she never confronted him about it."

"Maybe that's why Raymond left after Cora died. Maybe she found out, and he took off. Something brought him back here, though."

She told Lancaster about Raymond's daughter's plans for the house. "My guess is Catherine and Raymond had a disagreement today about the sale of the estate, and he killed her."

"Still doesn't explain why you came here tonight, or how you knew about this place." When Addison didn't respond, he added, "Let me guess. Catherine gave you the address."

Addison nodded.

"And you decided it was better to check it out all by yourself than tell me or anyone else about it," he said.

"It was a bad idea. I know. It's just ... when I was at the guesthouse tonight thinking about what happened to Catherine, I couldn't help it. I needed to know for myself."

"Well, I have to say, that's just about the stupidest reason I've ever heard. A better reason would have been because you and your family are all suspects in Catherine's murder and you were trying to clear your names."

He was right.

It was a better reason.

And she wished she'd thought of it.

CHAPTER 42

Addison sat on a chair on the porch the next morning, watching the sun's glorious rays pepper light across the horizon. She'd been worried to see Luke when she returned the night before, and though he was angry, he was relieved to know she was safe. It wasn't the way Addison had pictured their first week of marriage, and sometimes she wondered whether it was fair to hitch him to her wagon, dragging him along for an unpredictable ride.

With the truth of Joseph's disappearance coming to light, Addison thought Cora would feel resolved, anxious to reunite with Joseph after all this time. But Addison hadn't seen Cora since leaving Raymond's house the night before. In the past, she'd always helped spirits reunite and move on, but maybe this time was different. Maybe Cora had found her own way.

Marjorie stepped outside. "Mind if I join you?"

Addison smiled, "Sure."

"I've wanted to talk to you for a few days now, but the timing never seemed right."

"Is everything okay?"

"It will be. I want you to know how proud I am of you. You're strong, Addison. Much stronger than you give yourself credit for, and I've seen your strength increase a great deal over the last few years. It's one reason why I gave you the book."

One reason?

Is there another?

Marjorie pulled the book out of her handbag. "I hope you don't mind me borrowing it one last time. I want to show you something, to explain something to you before you discover it for yourself."

She felt uneasy, wondering what Marjorie would say.

Marjorie flipped to the back of the book, stopping three quarters of the way through. "Would you read this for me?"

"Aloud?"

"Doesn't matter. Read it to yourself, if you like."

Marjorie placed the book into Addison's lap, and Addison picked it up, poring over the words on the page. She snapped it closed when she finished. "I'm not sure what to make of it. Why did you want me to read this?"

"The other day when we were at the lookout point, you suspected I couldn't see Cora, and you were right. I can't see spirits at all anymore. I'd always thought it would feel like a blessing in the end, a relief for all the years I labored on their behalf, but you know something? It doesn't. It feels like a piece of my heart has been hollowed out."

The passage Addison had just read talked about a rite of passage, an event occurring just before the loss of life. "Are you telling me you ... you're going to—"

Marjorie nodded. "I don't know when, and it's nothing I want you to fret over, all right?"

"There must be something we can do, something to stop it from happening."

Marjorie grabbed Addison's hand, folding it between hers. "We all go sometime. With us, at least we get a bit of a warning beforehand. Fate chooses its time, and it isn't open for a bargain. Part of me wanted to keep it to myself, but I knew it wouldn't be right. So there it is, and here we are. Let's make the most of it, shall we?"

Tears pooled in Addison's eyes. She bit her lip, fighting to contain them. She understood, she just didn't accept. Marjorie was advancing in age, and she knew time was precious. She just assumed her gran still had years—not months or weeks or … days.

"I've lived a long life, dearest," Marjorie said. "A wonderful life. And after all these years I'm finally part of yours again, which is what I have always wanted."

"I know. It's just … you and Dad are the only family I have left."

"Not true. Luke is your family now, and the child you'll bear together is your family." Marjorie pressed a finger to the book. "And the wonderful thing is, you can use this to call on me when needed. Even if you don't see me, I'll be with you, watching over you, protecting you."

"I don't know how I'll do this without you."

"Of course you do. You're doing it now. Have faith in yourself, Addison. Remember the woman you became when you inherited the manor. She's the same woman sitting next to me today, only stronger."

Through blurry eyes, Addison watched Lancaster's squad car roll to a stop. She wiped her cheeks, doing her best to regain her composure. Lancaster exited first and headed straight to the guesthouse, asking to see Lia. Addison informed him she was inside. He nodded and went in.

Gene stepped out of the car next, looking tired and worn, much worse today than the day before. Addison and Marjorie walked over to meet him. He removed the house key from his jacket and stumbled up the porch stairs.

Catching Addison's eye, he stopped. "Well, I guess it's all over."

"What's all over?" Addison asked. "Did Raymond confess?"

Gene shook his head. "Well, no, but the police have found a knife inside a golf bag in his closet. I heard a deputy talking to Lancaster about it. There's dried blood on the knife. Guess O'Shea is running tests. He's the medical examiner for all of Suffolk County."

"I can't believe Raymond killed his own sister because she wanted to sell this place," Addison said.

"It was a waste, you know. He didn't stop anything from happening."

"What do you mean?"

"Catherine didn't just *want* to sell it," Gene said. "It's already sold."

CHAPTER 43

Prior to her death, Catherine had called a man named Harvey Caplan and given him the go ahead to purchase the estate. Caplan had been a guest of the manor and had told Catherine he liked the area so much he'd be willing to pay a substantial amount of money to purchase it if Catherine ever decided to sell. In recent weeks, papers had been drawn up and signed by both parties. In forty-five days he was to take ownership.

When Addison had overheard Raymond and Catherine arguing the day before, she assumed Catherine had told her brother of her deal with Caplan. Infuriated, he had killed her. Gene believed this to be true, but admitted to Addison that the night before when Raymond spoke to police, Raymond had a different story.

Raymond had admitted to seeing Catherine the day she died, but said he did so only to stop her from selling the estate. He believed after Cora's death, Cora's part of the estate went to him and that it was illegal for Catherine to sell it without his signature. Catherine produced a document to prove he was wrong, a letter

Cora had written prior to her suicide. In the letter, Cora stated her part of the estate was to go to Catherine. An argument ensued when Raymond accused Catherine of fabricating the letter and writing it herself, something Gene denied.

It was plausible to believe Raymond had killed his sister when she refused to stop the sale of the estate. But Raymond was old. Perhaps he plotted the crime but didn't commit the murder himself. It was possible he conspired with his daughter, and his daughter had dealt the fatal blow, later stashing the knife inside the golf bag. This theory was disproved when Lancaster said Raymond's daughter had an alibi. She had been at lunch with her fiancé over an hour away. Video surveillance provided by the restaurant confirmed it.

With the new evidence pointing to Raymond, Luke persuaded Lancaster to allow them to return to Rhinebeck. The decision left Addison with mixed feelings. There had been no closure with Cora, nothing to suggest she'd moved on, but there was nothing to suggest she still remained, either.

Bags were packed and loaded, and Addison watched Lia and Lancaster say goodbye, making plans to see each other again on the weekend.

Luke walked up, sliding his hand inside Addison's.

"I'm sorry," she said. "I should have been more straightforward with you last night."

He leaned in, kissing her cheek. "You didn't tell me because you knew what I would say. If you thought I would have been more supportive, you would have told me. I had a good talk with Marjorie yesterday. I'll try and do a better job of being there for you."

"I can do better too. And I will."

He smiled. "Ready to get out of here?"

Addison nodded. "I'd just like to say goodbye to Gene first."

"All right. I'll wait here with Marjorie. Thank him for me, would you?"

Addison stepped inside the manor, called out Gene's name. He didn't reply. She shouted his name a second time. Still nothing.

Whitney exited the kitchen, carrying a plate containing a sandwich and a green salad. "Is everything okay?"

"I was looking for Gene. I wanted to say goodbye."

"I think he went to his study. I was just taking him lunch. Follow me."

The thought of revisiting the spot where Catherine took her last breath made Addison squeamish. "Won't we have to go through Catherine's room to get there?"

"Oh, don't worry," Whitney said. "I know what you're thinking, and I've taken care of it."

Taken care of it?

It wasn't until they entered the bedroom that Addison understood her meaning. A thick, burgundy blanket had been spread over the area where Catherine died, concealing the bloodstains, but not the memory. The memory would remain forever.

"I can't stop Gene from reliving what happened here," Whitney said, "but until the floor is replaced, he doesn't need a constant reminder."

They entered the closet and stood at the top of the stairs.

"Gene, I have Addison with me," Whitney said. "We're coming down."

When Gene didn't reply, Whitney shrugged, and they walked in, finding him hunched over his desk. A bottle of whiskey rested a few inches in front of him next to an empty glass.

"Is he sleeping?" Addison whispered.

"Think so. After all he's been through, I don't blame him. He's exhausted."

"I don't want to wake him. Just tell him I said goodbye, okay?"

Whitney glanced at the food plate. "And I'll wrap this up for later. He probably doesn't have a big appetite right now, anyway."

Whitney leaned closer, reaching for the glass in front of him.

The plate slid off her hand, hurdling toward the floor. "Uhh …
Addison …?"

"What is it?"

Whitney lifted a piece of paper, holding it up for Addison to read.

Forgive me.

My life means nothing without Catherine.

CHAPTER 44

Addison felt for a pulse, but there was none. She turned to Whitney, shaking her head.

"No, no, no, no, no," Whitney said. "Not again. This can't be happening again."

"It may be different this time," Addison said. "Gene appears to have taken his own life."

Whitney lifted a cell phone out of the pocket of her apron. "I'll call the police."

"Good idea."

Addison's thought switched to something else—the method of his murder. There was no gunshot wound, no actual sign of injury. She studied Gene's desk. The top drawer was partially open. She reached for the handle and pulled it back, finding a small container about the size of a pill bottle tipped to the side over a stack of paper. It looked innocent enough, until she pulled it closer, inspecting the label.

"Police are on their way," Whitney said. "What did you find?"

Addison showed her the bottle. "Potassium cyanide."

Whitney clapped a hand over her mouth. "I can't believe he

would … it's unbelievable. I mean, I know he was grieving, but to end his life?"

On the wall across from Gene's desk were a series of framed drawings of trees, each one pertaining to a family member in the Blackthorn genealogical line. Addison gazed at each one, pausing when she looked at Joseph's. "Whitney, have you ever looked at these before?"

"Not really. I only know what Catherine told me."

Addison lifted Joseph's family tree off the wall and pointed to a name. "Do you know who this is?"

Whitney leaned in to get a better look. "Cameron. Yeah, I mean, I don't know much, but Catherine mentioned him to me once. It was on her birthday last year. It's one of the only times she ever allowed herself to drink. Two glasses of wine in, and she opened right up. I learned all kinds of things. It was actually how we bonded."

"What did she tell you about him?"

Before Whitney could answer, the sound of Luke's voice rang through the house. "Addison? Where are you?"

"Down here," Addison shouted, "in Gene's office."

Addison hung the picture frame back on the wall.

Her interrogation would have to wait.

She walked up the stairs, finding Luke and Colin in the hallway outside of Catherine's room.

"I didn't know Gene had an office," he said.

"I'll explain later. Right now, you need to see what's happened."

The three of them joined Whitney in Gene's office.

Addison pointed at Gene. "I don't think we'll be leaving yet, Luke. Gene's dead."

Frustrated, Luke whipped around. "What happened?"

"I don't know. We found him like this. There was a bottle of cyanide in his top drawer, which leads me to believe he wrote a suicide note and then poisoned his whiskey."

Colin wrapped his arms around a trembling Whitney, pulling her into an embrace.

"I know how much Gene loved Catherine," Colin said, "but I never thought he would take his own life."

"I thought the same thing," Whitney said.

Luke ran a hand down his face. "Well, I suppose we're not leaving then."

Addison shook her head. "I don't think we should. Not until we know what happened."

CHAPTER 45

Lancaster entered Gene's study with Marjorie in tow. The six of them stood around Gene, taking it all in.

"I'm beginning to think you don't want to leave as much as you say you do," Lancaster said. "It hasn't been more than thirty minutes since I left here. What is it with you people? And who wants to explain what happened this time?"

Addison volunteered, filling Lancaster in on how Gene was found, the suicide note, and the bottle she'd found inside his desk.

"This just doesn't feel right," Lancaster said. "I had a nice talk with Gene on the way here this morning. He told me after Catherine's funeral, he planned to live with his widowed sister in Harwich. If he wanted to kill himself, why would he go to the trouble of lying to me about it? He had nothing to gain."

CHAPTER 46

There was a small, but important detail Addison had overlooked, a comment Catherine had made in the vision Addison had the night she'd first met Billy.

She's under enough stress as it is, with the baby coming.

The baby.

How could she have forgotten?

The day of Joseph's disappearance Cora was pregnant, and not with Raymond's daughter. She wouldn't come until a couple of years later. Addison had never thought to ask what had become of Cora and Joseph's baby. Had he died? And if so, why had the date beneath his name on the family tree shown only a birth date and nothing else?

While Lancaster inspected the office, Addison went looking for Whitney. She found her by the ocean. Her arms were crossed in front of her, head bowed as if she was in prayer.

"Whitney, are you all right?" Addison asked.

Whitney's cheeks were sticky and red, her face damp with tears. "It finally felt like I had a family, you know? Like we had a family. And now it's all been stripped away."

"You still have Colin."

"Not just Colin."

"What do you mean?"

Whitney smoothed her dress over her abdomen, revealing the smallest swelling in her belly. "I'm three months pregnant. I mean, I never thought I could have a child at my age, or that I'd want a child again, but God has a different plan for me."

"That's great news. Does anyone else know?"

"Colin does, and now you. He's excited. We were planning on making a life here, but it wouldn't be the same now, not with Gene and Catherine both gone."

"Whitney, did you know Catherine planned to sell the manor?"

She nodded. "We talked about it a few times. She always said if she sold it, she'd make a side deal for the sale of the guesthouse so we could keep it if we wanted it. She'd actually made a deal with Harvey Caplan for us to buy the one and for her and Gene to keep the other. This way she'd still have access to the family gravesite while she was still living."

"I know you're hurting right now, and I'm sorry," Addison said. "I was hoping I could ask a few questions about Cameron, if you're up to it."

"I mean, I'm not, but it doesn't matter. What do you want to know?"

"Cora was pregnant with Cameron the day Joseph went out on his boat, right?"

Whitney shrugged. "I think so."

"What can you tell me about Cameron?"

"He lived at the manor until Cora committed suicide."

Addison thought back to the birth date she'd seen on the family tree. 1964. That meant he would have been five at the time of Cora's death. "What happened after her death?"

"Raymond left, taking the daughter he'd had with Cora, but because Cameron was his brother's child, he didn't consider him to be his, and he left him behind. Catherine woke to find a note from Raymond saying he'd gone and that Cameron was now her responsibility."

Addison assumed Raymond's reason for leaving the boy had more to do with his guilt over killing the boy's father than anything else. Keeping Cameron around would have been a constant reminder of his sin, a reminder he had endured while Cora was alive, but felt no longer obligated to after her death.

"Did Catherine and Gene raise Cameron, then?"

Whitney shook her head. "Catherine couldn't bear to be around children after Billy died, and even though it wasn't Cameron's fault, she just wasn't capable of raising him."

"What happened to Cameron then? Where is he?"

"Catherine had no other living family, so she asked Gene to find an orphanage, or somewhere Cameron could go and have a better life. The day Gene left with him she said she didn't want to know where he took him and never wanted to speak of it again."

"One last question," Addison said. "How long has the gardener been working here?"

Whitney looked up, thinking. "Brad? Two or three months. The previous gardener just stopped showing up one day."

"Where did she find Brad?"

Whitney considered the question. "You know something—I don't know."

CHAPTER 47

If Addison wanted to know what happened to Cameron, she needed to talk to someone who knew the story. With Catherine and Gene dead, Raymond in jail, Lancaster hard at work trying to figure out whether Gene's death was a murder or a suicide, there was only one other person who might have the answers she needed —Lancaster's father.

Addison was reluctant to leave Marjorie, but Marjorie encouraged her, saying after all that had gone on over the past few days, she'd rather stay back and relax.

When Luke and Addison arrived, they hadn't even made it to the door before it opened.

"Can I help you two?" the man asked.

"Are you Lyle Lancaster?"

"Depends. Who are you?"

"I'm Addison, and this is my husband, Luke. We're staying at Blackthorn Manor."

Directing his attention to Addison, he said, "Ahh. You must be the troublemaker my son has been telling me about. What are you doing here?"

"Have you talked to your son today?"

"If you're asking if I know Gene's dead, I do. My son texted me. And if you're asking whether or not he killed himself, he didn't."

"Has your son found something?"

"Not yet, but he will."

"I don't believe Gene took his own life, either," Addison said. "Over the past few days, I've learned a lot about the Blackthorn family history. There's one thing I'm curious about, and I think you might be the only one who can answer my questions."

Lyle laughed. "My son said you like to be in the middle of things."

"She doesn't," Luke said. "All she wants to do is—"

Lyle waved a hand in front of him. "Now calm down there, son. No need to get cross. I'm not making an accusation."

He turned, disappearing into the house, leaving Addison and Luke standing outside, wondering what to do next.

"He left the door open," Addison said. "Do you think we're supposed to follow him?"

Luke shook his head. "I don't know. He's kinda hard to read."

Lyle's voice echoed outside. "I've got pasta cooking on the stove. You two lovebirds coming in, or what?"

CHAPTER 48

"What is it I can help you with?" Lyle asked.

Addison hadn't heard the question. She was too busy gawking at Lyle's living room. The walls were plain and white, his mahogany hardwood floor polished, with furniture consisting of a brown leather sofa and matching chair. A flat-screen TV befitting a man who lived alone hung on the wall, but it was the items across from it that captured her attention. Clocks. And not just one clock. Dozens of them spread out across the wall.

"Addison," Luke said, "Lyle asked you a question."

She faced Lyle. "Yeah … sorry. Interesting collection of clocks."

His face beamed with delight. "Over the years I've brought one clock back from every significant place I've been to in my life. If you look closely, you'll notice the times are all different, set in the time of the place where they came from. It's a fun little hobby. Drives my son nuts, though. He says he'll chuck them one day when I'm not around anymore, but he won't."

Lyle pushed two cans of soda in front of Addison and Luke. "Who's going to tell me what you're doing here?"

Cut to the chase.

Like father, like son.

"I wanted to ask you about Cameron Blackthorn, Joseph and Cora's baby," Addison said.

"Cameron? What about him?"

"I understand Gene took him somewhere after Cora's death."

He nodded. "That's right."

"And Catherine never knew where."

"I suppose she thought if she didn't know, it would ease her guilt somehow. But I don't think it ever did. I understand why she couldn't raise him, but to turn him out the way they did when he was heartsick over his mother ... well, I always thought it was a brutal thing to do to a young boy."

"Do you know where Gene took him?"

He turned to the stove, giving the pasta a quick stir. "You two wanna have a seat at the bar?"

They sat down.

"Gene was going to send the boy to his sister's house at first," he said. "She had never been able to have children of her own, and she was thrilled about the idea. Gene's concern for how Catherine would feel about it got the better of him, though, and he ended up taking him to a foster agency."

"Which one?"

"I'm not sure. He didn't say. But I do know that for the first couple of years he saw Cameron on occasion in secret. I suppose I was probably the only one who knows that information."

"Why you?"

Lyle took a moment, then said, "I felt bad for the boy, so I tried to foster him myself."

"What happened?"

"Gene begged me not to—said Catherine would lose her mind once it got around town. It would make it look like she'd abandoned him. I didn't think it would have made a difference.

People already thought it, and they weren't keen on her, anyway. When I spoke to the agency, they said I couldn't foster him because he was in a different county, and only people living in that county could foster him. Stupid rule, if you ask me, but that's how it was back then."

"Before Cora died, were you ever around Cameron?"

"A few times."

"What did he look like?" Addison asked.

"He was a good-looking kid. He had big, bright eyes like his mother, and pale-blond hair. It was so fair it almost looked white. And then when he was a toddler, he fell outside, hit his head on a rock, leaving him with a scar, a two-inch gash over his right eye."

Luke and Addison exchanged glances.

"What is it?" Lyle asked.

"We have to go. I'm sorry."

"Now wait a minute. I gave you information, now you can do the same."

"Raymond may be responsible for Joseph's death," Addison said, "but I don't believe he killed Catherine."

"Why not? What do you know that suggests otherwise?"

"I've seen the scar you described, only it isn't on a little boy anymore. It's on a man."

"What are you suggesting?"

Addison shot out of the chair. "Call your son. Tell him what we talked about and that we're headed back to the manor. If he's not still there, he needs to be."

CHAPTER 49

I've seen that look before," Luke said. "You're plotting. You need to let Lancaster handle it."

"I will," Addison said.

"I mean it."

"I know, and I will. Besides, we're together now. You're with me. Nothing is going to happen."

Addison tried calling Marjorie, but there was no answer, making her uneasy. Marjorie had promised to leave her phone on. So why hadn't she picked up?

They arrived at the Blackthorn estate at dusk. All was quiet, eerily so, the only sound made by crickets rubbing their wings together, chirping.

"Where is everyone?" Luke asked. "Where's Lancaster?"

"I'm worried about Marjorie," Addison said. "I shouldn't have left her."

"She said she was going to rest," Luke said. "She's probably sleeping."

Addison and Luke entered the guesthouse, finding Marjorie sleeping peacefully on the bed.

"Told you," Luke said. "She's fine. She just needed some rest."

Marjorie's eyelids opened halfway. "And you two are preventing it, so if you don't mind …"

"Sorry, Gran," Addison said. "We were just checking on you. I tried calling."

Marjorie sighed and reached for her phone. "Huh. So I see."

"Gran, I need to communicate with Cora."

"Why don't you just summon her?"

"If she's moved on, I'm not sure I can."

"I'm willing to bet she's still here. I wouldn't waste time. You need to find out. The sooner the better."

"Will you join me?"

"Not this time. It's up to you now."

Addison leaned over, kissing her grandmother on the forehead, and then walked out of the room.

"How can I help?" Luke asked.

"I need to get inside the manor, into Billy's room."

"Why?"

"Because it used to be Cora's once," Addison said.

"I'm guessing it's all locked up."

Addison opened her hand, dangling a key from her finger.

"Is that …?"

Addison nodded.

"Where did you get it?" Luke asked.

"Top drawer of Gene's study."

He shook his head but said nothing.

"I need to do this alone, Luke."

"I'm not letting you out of my sight right now, Addison. No way."

"I just need you to stand outside the room until I've done what I need to do."

She inserted the key into the manor's front door. They climbed the stairs, and walked into the bedroom. Luke glanced around, making sure no one else was present. "All right. I'll be on the other side of this door if you need me."

Addison sat on the floor, crossing one leg over the other. She closed her eyes and concentrated on her breathing, creating stillness within. She focused on every curve of Cora's face, creating a vision in her mind, a perfect picture that started to blend, the image of Cora distorting, transforming into someone else—Joseph.

"Cora, I command you to appear."

Tiny slivers of delicate, glittery light swirled in front of Addison, like sand collecting, forming a figure, and within it, Cora took shape.

"Hi, Cora," Addison said.

Cora scanned the room, searching.

"He will come," Addison said. "Trust me."

Addison picked Joseph's necklace out of her pocket, clutching it inside her hand. "Joseph Blackthorn, I command *you* to appear."

The wall lit up, parting like a large, circular portion had been sucked out of the middle. A bright, beaming ball of light circled, bending and twisting into the form of a man. Joseph appeared in the room, and the wall became normal again. He blinked at Addison and then turned toward Cora. His face softened, his chest pounding inside his body, the weight of decades apart finally coming to an end.

He reached for Cora's hand, and she smiled, finally able to let go. Addison expected Cora to run to him, to leap into his arms. Instead, she turned toward Addison.

"I know why you haven't left yet, Cora," Addison said. "You're worried about your son, aren't you?"

Cora nodded. "Bring … him … to … me."

"I know the truth now, why he did what he did, and I know you're hurting because of it. You wanted me to bring him to you before he hurts anyone else."

Again, Cora nodded.

"Let me handle him." Addison said. "Trust me, okay? I need you to go with Joseph now."

Joseph reached out a second time. As Cora floated in his direction, a strange sensation hit Addison, an odd, yet familiar smell. Smoke, permeating her lungs, spilling through the cracks around the door and into the room.

The manor was on fire.

CHAPTER 50

The door thrust open, but it wasn't Luke who entered. Addison coughed into her sweater, her head shaking furiously. "No! Get out of here! Get away from me! Stay back!"

Addison screamed for Luke, only then noticing his body toppled over on the floor. "Luke!"

"Luke, Luke, please! Get up!" She glared at Colin, who she now knew as Cameron. "What did you do to him?"

"I didn't mean for this to happen," Cameron said. "Not to you and your family. You just, you were all here at the wrong time. I had to, don't you see? I hate this place, and everyone in it."

Addison bolted toward the door.

Cameron grabbed her arm, snapping it back.

"Let me go!" Addison screamed.

"I told Whitney tonight. I told her everything. I couldn't stand seeing her in so much pain. I thought she would understand once I explained. I thought she loved me. But she's gone. She left me, Addison."

Lancaster's voice boomed from outside the house. "Addison! Luke! Are you in there?"

"We're here!" Addison yelled. "Upstairs. Hurry!"

The fire was spreading.

If she didn't find a way out fast, she'd be dead.

They would all be dead.

She wriggled a hand free from Cameron's grasp, wrapping her fingers around a statue on the nightstand. She thrust it forward, smashing it into Cameron's head. He tumbled to the floor, taking her with him. She kicked him off of her and came to her knees.

She turned back.

Cameron moved—he was still alive.

Cora and Joseph hovered over their son. Cora lifted a finger at Addison, pointing toward the door. "Go. Now."

Keeping her head down low, Addison crawled to Luke. Blood seeped from a small wound on the side of his head. She wrapped her arms around his chest, dragging him toward the stairs, her breathing growing more and more shallow as precious seconds ticked by. Through a small break in the flames, she saw Lancaster pulling himself through a shattered window. He looked up and saw Addison, swooped his arms toward himself.

"Just get to me. You can do it!"

But she couldn't.

Every bit of air she sucked in made her weaker than the last, only adding to the intense burning sensation in her throat. Using what little energy she had remaining, she slid Luke onto the stairs and gave him a push, hoping the tumble he was about to take would save his life and not end it.

Lancaster stumbled over to him.

"Get him out of here!" Addison screamed. "He's hurt."

Not wanting to leave Addison behind, Lancaster paused, but then nodded. "I'll be right back for you. You hang on, Addison—you hear me?"

CHAPTER 51

Suffocating, Addison slumped to the floor, accepting the truth of her situation. Spirits may not have had the power to end her life, but humans did.

This is it.

This is the end.

My end.

The stairs are caving in.

Lancaster will never make it in time.

The sound of her grandmother's boisterous, commanding voice sliced through the dense air. "Addison … open your eyes."

It isn't possible.

How can she be here?

She can't be.

Addison's eyes stung like salt had been poured into them. Opening them would only make it worse. But she had to. She parted her eyelids, finding Marjorie looming over her.

"How are you here?" Addison asked.

"Never mind, dearest. I need you to crawl for me. Crawl down the first few stairs, and I'll do the rest. Come on, now."

Addison pressed her palms into the floor, willing herself to get up.

Arms shaky and weak, her first attempt did nothing. She glanced at the first step of the staircase. It was less than a foot away. One foot seemed like one mile. She gritted her teeth, tried again, inching.

Almost … there.

A beam crashed to the floor.

The house was caving in around her.

"Reach for me!" Marjorie said. "Take my hand. Take it now."

Addison pushed toward Marjorie until their hands connected, and Addison felt herself being lifted, carried downstairs. The smoke too thick and heavy for Addison to see, she had nothing but her grandmother's soothing words to guide her.

"You're going to be fine. You're safe now. And remember, I'll always be here when you need me."

CHAPTER 52

Addison woke to find herself strapped to a gurney inside an ambulance. Luke was beside her, the top of his head covered in a bandage which made him look like an 80s rock star. He noticed Addison blinking at him and leaned over, kissing both of her cheeks.

"I'm glad you're awake," he said.

Addison tugged at the ventilator over her mouth. Luke placed a hand over it.

"Leave it on, okay?" Luke said.

Addison shook her head, pushing it to the side. "What happened?"

"I'll tell you if you put it back on."

"Just tell me, Luke."

"It looks like Colin started the fire. Before I could get to it, he clocked me. When I came to, I was being pushed through the window and Lancaster was going back inside for you."

"Gran got me out. How is she?"

Luke looked confused. "Lancaster rescued you. He burned his hand and part of his leg doing it."

"Gran was there though. She told me to take her hand, and she pulled me down the stairs."

"You may have thought it was her, but it wasn't."

"I didn't *think* it was her. I saw her, Luke."

Luke ran a finger along her arm. "Can you please put the ventilator back on? Once we get to the hospital, we can talk more about it."

"I want to know now. Where is she? Is she all right?"

"After the firemen got to the house, Lancaster went to check on Marjorie. She was still in bed. He tapped her on the shoulder, but she didn't wake up. He rolled her over and noticed … well, she wasn't breathing. It looks like she passed away in her sleep."

CHAPTER 53

A soft glow filtered through the slats dressing the hospital window, casting shapes of light onto Addison's face. Luke snored on a chair next to her. The day before seemed like a blur, a horrible nightmare that wasn't real. Except it *was* real, and Gran was gone, just like she said she would be.

A tapping sound sprung Luke from the chair next to Addison's bed. Bleary-eyed, he went to the hospital room door and opened it. Whitney entered carrying an armful of flowers.

"I hope it's okay for me to stop by," she said. "If it's not, I can just leave these and go."

"Come in," Addison said.

"I wanted to check on you, see how you were doing."

Addison turned toward Luke. "Can you give us a few minutes?"

"Sure, I'll, uhh, run down to the cafeteria and get something to eat," he said. "Want anything?"

Addison shook her head. "I'm not sure I can handle food right now."

He nodded and left the room.

"I just want to say how sorry I am," Whitney said. "I think about how blind I've been. I can look back now and see hints of things here and there, warnings I should have heeded, but I was swept up in the fairy tale, you know? And I thought he was it. I really did. And now, on top of everything else, I'll always wonder how much was the truth and how much was a lie."

Addison slid a hand down the side of the bed and pushed on the control button, propping her up to a sitting position. "He didn't just lie to you. He lied to everyone."

She glanced out the window, her voice quivering. "They found him this morning. He was ... there wasn't much left of him."

Addison believed Cora's longing for Joseph wasn't the only reason she'd stuck around so long. Her guilt played a part—the guilt of a mother abandoning her son—and for what became of him following her death.

"He may have been out for revenge," Addison said, "but I believe he loved you."

"You think so? I don't know how a person who did what he did is capable of loving anyone. He used me to become involved in their lives, all the while planning their murders."

"What he did was wrong. But I've tried to imagine what he went through at such a young age. His mother died, and then he was cast out. If not for that, I bet he would have grown up to be a lot different than he did."

"I see what you're saying, but you don't go on a killing spree because you've hated people all your life. It doesn't make it okay." She glanced at her stomach. "And now I'm having his baby. What am I supposed to say? How am I supposed to explain? And what if my child turns out to be like him?"

"You just need to love your child. And if you want my opinion, there's no rush to explain anything. When the time is right, you'll know what to say."

Whitney sat on a chair, folding her arms in her lap. "He confessed everything, you know. He honestly thought once he explained it all, I wouldn't see him as a bad person."

"What I don't understand is why did he choose to do it now, after all this time?"

"Harvey Caplan raised Colin, I mean, Cameron, from the age of twelve. He was wealthy, an investment banker from what Catherine told me. Some time back, he stayed at the manor. He wanted to know what Catherine and Gene were like. He also made them the offer to buy the estate. He'd intended on giving it to Cameron, but at the time, Catherine wasn't ready to sell."

"When did Cameron find out about Harvey's plans?"

Whitney crossed one leg over the other. "The first time Harvey visited, he told Cameron he wanted to purchase it for him. I believe it stirred something up in Cameron, and he started reliving what had happened all those years ago. It wasn't enough for him to own the estate. He blamed them for everything—his father's death, his mother's, and for rejecting him. He wanted the Ravencrofts to pay for what they had done."

"All this time, Catherine and Gene had no idea who Colin really was—how did it remain a secret?"

"Cameron told Harvey he didn't think Catherine would sell the estate if she knew who he was, so they decided to keep quiet until the deal was done. Harvey wanted justice for Cameron after all he'd suffered, but I don't think he knew what Cameron was planning."

"And last night he confessed Catherine's and Gene's murders to you?"

Whitney nodded.

Addison thought back to the beginning, to when she'd first arrived at the manor. "It was Cameron who pushed me out the bedroom window, right?"

"Yes."

CHERYL BRADSHAW

"Why?"

"He was paranoid. He told me he thought you caught him snooping around Catherine's room the morning of your wedding."

It was his imagination. She'd seen nothing. "I didn't. I was in my room until I fell."

"I was walking by Catherine's room that morning. He said he had only caught a glimpse of a woman, and he probably mistook me for you."

"What about the day Catherine died? You said he was with you at the store."

She looked down. "Yeah, I know. I shouldn't have said that. He wasn't."

"Why did you lie?"

"He was waiting outside for me when I arrived. He said something horrible had happened to Catherine, and everyone was being questioned. He said he was worried they'd suspect him since he was alone in the guesthouse at the time, and I didn't see any reason not to say he was with me. I was sure he wasn't responsible for her death."

Luke entered the room carrying two cups of coffee. He held one out to Whitney, "Thought you might like one."

She accepted it and stood. "I would—thanks. I need to go, though. I just wanted to say how sorry I was to hear about Marjorie."

"And we're sorry for how things ended up with Colin … I mean … Cameron," Addison said. "What will you do now?"

She shrugged. "I just know I need to leave here. It's time for another fresh start."

Whitney walked out of the room, passing the doctor who was on his way in, an older man in his seventies with crooked front teeth and a substantial mustache.

The doctor smiled at Addison. "Glad you're awake. How are you feeling today?"

"All right, I guess."

194

"It's a miracle you both made it out of there. If it wasn't for Lancaster … well, we don't need to go into the what-ifs of it all. I'm sure you both know how lucky you are."

"How is he?" Addison asked.

"Oh, fine. Tough as a bear, that one. Nothing he can't handle."

"Can we see him?"

"Sure. I believe your friend is with him now—Lia I think she said her name was." He paused, then said, "You're probably wondering how your tests came back, so let me put you both at ease. Everything looks good. The little one is just fine."

Addison and Luke exchanged glances.

"The *little one*?" Addison asked.

The doctor smiled and patted Addison's stomach. "Heartbeat is strong and fast, just like it should be at six weeks. I see nothing to worry about. Your baby is in perfect health."

CHAPTER 54

One Month Later

Hand in hand, Addison and Luke stood in front of Marjorie's grave, marveling at the lavish, marble tombstone erected at her burial site. Prior to her death, Marjorie had taken care of everything, leaving detailed instructions on where she was to be buried and of her desire to be cremated. She'd even taken the time to order a tombstone. In her will, she left everything to Addison, which was a greater sum than Addison realized her grandmother had amassed over the years.

Standing in front of Marjorie's grave now, it was still difficult for Addison to accept she'd never see her grandmother again, but it comforted her to know that in the end, Marjorie had returned to protect her. Over the last few weeks, Addison had read through the black book, reading every entry multiple times until she'd committed them to memory. She would continue to honor her legacy, and she'd strive to make her grandmother proud.

"Marjorie Jane Grayson," Luke said. "I never knew her middle name was the same as yours."

"Same as my mother's too," Addison said. "It's a tradition."

He rubbed Addison's belly and smiled. "So I guess we'll be using it on this little one if she's a girl."

"She is a girl."

He smiled. "Oh, really? You seem confident."

"Gran knew about her before we did," Addison said. "She told me I was going to have a girl."

"When?"

"The night of our wedding when we walked along the beach. I didn't believe her at first because we had decided to wait. I thought there was no way I could be pregnant."

"Are you disappointed it's happening so soon?"

Addison shook her head. "I can't wait to be a mother. You?"

"I don't know why, but the timing seems perfect now, but surreal. We're mourning the loss of a life while celebrating a new one at the same time."

Addison bent down, placing a bouquet of white lilies in front of the headstone.

"Ready to go?" he asked.

She nodded, and they turned, walking back to the car. A gentle breeze kicked up, and within it a voice as soft and sweet as a whisper, and she swore she heard a name—Amara.

Amara Jane.

It had a nice ring to it.

THE END

The End

ABOUT CHERYL BRADSHAW

Cheryl Bradshaw is a *New York Times* and *USA Today* bestselling author writing in the genres of mystery, thriller, paranormal suspense, and romantic suspense. Her novel *Stranger in Town* (Sloane Monroe series #4) was a 2013 Shamus Award finalist for Best PI Novel of the Year, and her novel *I Have a Secret* (Sloane Monroe series #3) was a 2013 eFestival of Words winner for best thriller. Since 2013, Five of Cheryl's novels have made the *USA Today* bestselling books list.

BOOKS BY CHERYL BRADSHAW

Sloane Monroe Series

Black Diamond Death (Book 1)

Charlotte Halliwell has a secret. But before revealing it to her sister, she's found dead.

Murder in Mind (Book 2)

A woman is found murdered, the serial killer's trademark "S" carved into her wrist.

I Have a Secret (Book 3)

Doug Ward has been running from his past for twenty years. But after his fourth whisky of the night, he doesn't want to keep quiet, not anymore.

Stranger in Town (Book 4)

A frantic mother runs down the aisles, searching for her missing daughter. But little Olivia is already gone.

Bed of Bones (Book 5)

Sometimes even the deepest, darkest secrets find their way to the surface.

Flirting with Danger (Book 5.5) A Sloane Monroe Short Story

A fancy hotel. A weekend getaway. For Sloane Monroe, rest has finally arrived, until the lights go out, a woman screams, and Sloane's nightmare begins.

Hush Now Baby (Book 6)

Serena Westwood tiptoes to her baby's crib and looks inside, startled to find her newborn son is gone.

Dead of Night (Book 6.5) A Sloane Monroe Short Story

After her mother-in-law is fatally stabbed, Wren is seen fleeing with the bloody knife. Is Wren the killer, or is a dark, scandalous family secret to blame?

Gone Daddy Gone (Book 7)

A man lurks behind Shelby in the park. Who is he? And why does he have a gun?

Sloane Monroe Stories: Deadly Sins

Deadly Sins: Sloth (Book 1)

Darryl has been shot, and a mysterious woman is sprawled out on the floor in his hallway. She's dead too. Who is she? And why have they both been murdered?

Deadly Sins: Wrath (Book 2)

Headlights flash through Maddie's car's back windshield, someone following close behind. When her car careens into nearby tree, the chase comes to an end. But for Maddie, the end is just the beginning.

Addison Lockhart Series

Grayson Manor Haunting (Book 1)

When Addison Lockhart inherits Grayson Manor after her mother's untimely death, she unlocks a secret that's been kept hidden for over fifty years.

Rosecliff Manor Haunting (Book 2)

Addison Lockhart jolts awake. The dream had seemed so real. Eleven-year-old twins Vivian and Grace were so full of life, but they couldn't be. They've been dead for over forty years.

Blackthorn Manor Haunting (Book 3)

Addison Lockhart leans over the manor's window, gasping when she feels a hand on her back. She grabs the windowsill to brace herself, but it's too late--she's already falling.

Till Death do us Part Novella Series

Whispers of Murder (Book 1)

It was Isabelle Donnelly's wedding day, a moment in time that should have been the happiest in her life...until it ended in murder.

Echoes of Murder (Book 2)

When two women are found dead at the same wedding, medical examiner Reagan Davenport will stop at nothing to discover the identity of the killer.

Stand-Alone Novels

Eye for Revenge
Quinn Montgomery wakes to find herself in the hospital. Her childhood best friend Evie is dead, and Evie's four-year-old son witnessed it all. Traumatized over what he saw, he hasn't spoken.

The Devil Died at Midnight
When true-crime writer Alexandria Weston is found murdered on the last stop of her book tour, fellow writer Joss Jax steps in to investigate.

Hickory Dickory Dead
Maisie Fezziwig wakes to a harrowing scream outside. Curious, she walks outside to investigate, and Maisie stumbles on a grisly murder that will change her life forever.

76120940R00116